MOIRA'S SACRIFICE

MOIRA'S SACRIFICE

'simple stories are the best'

By

KEN ROSS

More Ken Ross novels:

The Lads Will Have Blood (Crime Thriller).

A Cross of Crocuses (Family Saga).

ANN: irresistible spirit (Romance)

An Old Affair (Romance)

KEN ROSS Romantic/Erotic Suspense Series: Wasted Pain, Protection, Bodies, Mama, Broken Sisters & Goodbye Violet.

Rosalee's Punishment (Erotic Suspense).

Louann's Home Movie (Erotic Suspense).

The Last Days of Childhood (Young Adult)

Wrapped in Green Comfort (Literary Fiction)

Rosa's Confessions (Erotic Suspense Series): Superfluous, Partial Absolution, Happiness Regained, Lizzie & Moira's Sacrifice.

MOIRA'S SACRIFICE

When the bruises healed

I swore to use this opening line even though it's not truthful. The
vibrators may be gathering dust, but they're still here. So here is the
line: 'We took a box full of vibrators to the charity shop along with
two unused flowery pillowcases and an unopened box of Ferrero
Rocher.' It made me laugh, and God, these days there's little to laugh
about.

Only a few weeks have passed since Lizzie left my body
purple, blue, green, mauve, black, yellow, and bloody red. I survived
the worst battering of my life and live on to tell the tale. The
outcome is ghastly. Worse than ghastly, days are sexless, and
communication relates to meals, cleaning, shifts at the café, and
polite phrases such as 'excuse me'. Our house has become a place
where clothed bodies are the norm, and when I take off my bra and
knickers to establish if I'm still nakedly attractive, I feel like a freak.

So... updates. Let's start with Lizzie. I was accused of
enacting the most insane gesture of my life when I invited Lizzie to
come and live with us. We'd healed Tracey's injured leg after her fall
from the harness at the sex club, got rid of her limp with lots of
massages, exercises, sex, love, and care, so I saw no reason why we
couldn't cure Lizzie of her pyromaniac propensity – that's a sensitive
way of she's been an arsonist who burned her parents alive in their
beds.

'What!' implored Tracey at the time.
'Are you off your trolley?' asked Moira at the time.
'You can't do that!' yelled Marty at the time.
And my sister Katy was doubly outraged.

I remember gathering them in the room and saying how fortunate we are to have such wonderful lives, happily screwing one another (well, occasionally), and saying folks like us have a duty to those less privileged. We have money, possessions, love, and wake up every morning with a purpose to reach bedtime not specifically to sleep. Lizzie has been living with her uncle who rescued her from the fire; she's been living with a mountain of guilt on her shoulders, and she doesn't know how to have a normal relationship. She desperately needs a psychiatrist, and as she can't go visit one and confess her crime, then I'm the only soul on earth who can cure her – or attempt to cure her. 'What would you all do?' I asked. 'Cast her into a world where the only job that would suit her is working at a crematorium?'

Lizzie had tortured me during a sex act. Marty came to my rescue, and subsequently, I punched Lizzie in the mouth, had her cowering in a corner fearing for her life before she came out with the news of her secret murders many years previously. Surely, to right-minded folk, that's a girl who merits attention, and is worthy of pity?

Tracey, Moira, Marty, and Katy all put their thumbs down. I said we had a spare bedroom. 'Had I a desire to be toasted?' I said we'd ban lighters, matches, and any device that can produce a flame from the house. Tracey pointed out that the cooker lights with a button. I promised to sleep on the sofa and keep an all-night watch on the kitchen door. 'Who throws screwed-up kids into society? She'll return to her Russian uncle and boil him in a stew-pan – do you want that on your conscience?'

Hell, that day after the beating and the confession I argued Lizzie's case for the best part of six hours. I kept showing my girls, Katy and Marty, my multi-colored body and saying if I could forgive her, then what's the big problem. And then I slipped up. I speculated that if Lizzie could be cured of her evil tendencies (firelighting and violent sex) then imagine what she could contribute to orgies – who's got a body like hers? We could share her – she'd be a pleasure zone for the foreseeable future. I got accused of selfishness and had to retract the statement. 'You know me, I'm joking,' I said, 'I won't be using her if I'm sleeping on the sofa.'

Unbelievably, the person who paved the way for a breakthrough was Moira. My sweet little orphaned maid Moira started to relate what it was like having no parents as a child. Moira had always felt like a child, and that's why when I paid her attention when I first lifted her dress outside the SMA building, she clung to me. Moira admitted that she loves me just as she'd love a real Mum – maybe Lizzie similarly looks on me in that way. Rosa Saint John has two huge wings and she is capable of sheltering a young girl under each.

Tracey's got a heart as big as a cabbage and she was the first after Moira to soften her stance. 'A trial week,' she proffered, 'any sign of violence or nastiness, and she's gone.'

Katy hesitantly said she'd help in any way she could but her knowledge of headcases is limited to my behavior over the past two years. Marty timidly went along with Katy – he was creeping because he hadn't got a genuine excuse for calling at my house that fateful evening; all of us knew he'd popped in with the hope of screwing me while Tracey and Moira were in London for the weekend, but nobody said anything.

So… by Sunday evening, all fire-making devices apart from the cooker had been disposed of and a bed was prepared in the third bedroom for super-sexy but deranged Lizzie.

Was I bubbling with joy when my wish to ensconce Lizzie in our three-bedroomed semi was granted? Hell no! Folks may say I'm a raving sex-maniac and that my sexual urges should be quelled with a spoonful or two of arsenic, but the truth is that compassion is my weakness and when I see a young girl well off the rails, I know she's screaming for help, and it's my goddamn duty as a female to help her. I guess it wasn't exactly fair on Moira, but in time, she'll understand. As for Tracey, who for months now, hasn't been a raving nymphomaniac, she'd go along with it providing that Lizzie doesn't jeopardize our three-way relationship (me, her, and Moira). And Katy, I longed to show my sister that I had no interest in stealing back Marty irrespective of his continuing desire to get his hands on my body. Foolishly, a part of me thought that taking in Lizzie would restore Katy's trust in my ex. Anyhow, step one after the slaughter, involved clearing out the third bedroom and making it comfortable for our new resident.

Early days

Naively, I expected a day or two to pass with a few awkward moments destroying the 100% harmony. In reality, the 100% awkwardness passed with a few moments of harmony – and those moments came when we were all asleep. Madly, none of us slept for long; I think Tracey and Moira kept watch on their bedroom doors fearing a lighted rag would be slotted under the lowest gap. Lizzie probably tossed and turned and believed I may creep into her new bedroom with a plan for revenge fresh formed in my mind. And me, God, I laid awake for many hours half convinced that my sex-life was over; I didn't dare ask Tracey to relieve me; smuggling my body beneath Moira's duvet was out of the question, and if I touched Lizzie my girls would have booked me a cell in an asylum considering what she'd already done to me.

Those first days were odd because Katy and Marty seemed to call at every opportunity; they'd leave my sister's daughters with our parents and turn up out of the blue. And it wasn't for a conversation that they'd sit on the sofa casting their eyes at Tracey, Moira, Lizzie, and me, at least on Katy's part, it was to assess the state of play. Despite me telling her that nothing is going on between me and Marty, she needed to convince herself that my eyes weren't straying in his direction. She had no acceptable answer as to why he turned up that night to rescue me. She needed to feel the vibes and felt compelled to quantify the trust to place in both me and Marty. I really can't say why her interest extended to my girls. Yes, she'd always been fond of Moira and perhaps wanted to establish my level of neglect – was I shoving Moira away to get my claws deep into Lizzie's luscious flesh? Maybe Katy believed the relationship between Tracey and I would suffer and she had ideas of being some kind of counselor. I've got to say no matter how hard Marty tried to conceal his guilt, he failed. Every time I passed him, he glanced at my ass then swiftly pretended to be looking elsewhere.

One observation from the early days did bother me. I'm sure, without exception, my nearest and dearest were convinced I had feelings for Lizzie. Perhaps only Tracey knew me well enough to accept that the significance of Lizzie's body was my overriding concern; Tracey could see what I saw in her – an irresistible delight to give favors and receive favors in return, and Tracey in her former days would have gorged in such succulence. But Moira, Katy, and Marty, and perhaps Lizzie too, thought that because I'd welcomed her into my home, I was falling in love. I'd get annoyed by wondering how anyone with a grain of sense could think I'd fallen for Lizzie.

Lizzie, bar none, is the most unlovable creature walking the face of the earth. That's not to say that the possibility of change is unconscionable, but from the outset, she's been a thoroughbred bitch whose heart is a stone and lovability is non-existent. Until Lizzie cowered in the corner of my bedroom, I'd even argue that she is not human.

As I've said, Lizzie stole my compassion and snatched a bagful of pity from my soul. I'm morally bound to help her. If at all possible, sometime soon I'd dearly love to have sex with her, but as for loving her, it's a misconception. I haven't bothered to explain my feelings to anyone for if I bring up the topic, I'll be falsely accused of building a secret relationship with a girl I purport to find characteristically distasteful.

After a few days of recovering from my wounds, I resumed my shifts at the café with Tracey and Lizzie. In these early days, Moira appeared reluctant to leave the house. I got the impression she had notions that Lizzie may miraculously toss a bomb from the café doorway all the way to the house and we'd return to a pile of rubble which would include the broken remains of her laptop. Moira wished to keep guard and the café counter proved less alluring than her bedroom.

Working with Tracey and Lizzie brought more awkwardness. Tracey's one topic is business; Lizzie's sole aim is to hide the person she's been since birth, and I'm left playing the role of an efficient bacon & egg server when I'd normally be firing out sexual innuendoes at least once a minute. 'Pass me a can from the cooler, please.' 'Better collect those greasy plates.' 'Have we enough milk?' 'The man wearing the cap hasn't yet paid.' Jesus, this is the consequence of allowing my lesbian apprentice to strap me on the bed and batter my body with an eighteen-inch dildo.

Four girls in a house

In some ways, I'm mightily stubborn. It's a lie to state that I instantly got used to being fully attired in the comfort of my home. Ever since Marty left me, I've luxuriated in the pleasure of walking about naked, or in just my underwear. I can't say how many hours I've stood near the front windows exhibiting my tits and giving passing old men seizures. And at my bedroom window, I shock flying birds with my solo exploits. I've gone into the rear garden naked, laid on the bench, and the grass, and the hundreds of times I've been naughty on the kitchen table are incalculable. It's the norm for me to be naked or in a bathrobe with nothing beneath. However, since Lizzie's occupancy of the third bedroom, a dress code is called for. Disapproving eyes say I shouldn't be permanently on display.

'Do you want Moira thinking you're going upstairs for a session with Lizzie?'

'Do you want Tracey to suggest having sex with Lizzie or Moira?' She isn't going to.

'Do you want Lizzie to believe she's cured and forgiven?'

Keep your clothes on, girl. Sex has been abolished. If you want sex take yourself off to the garden shed and close the door when you're inside.

We became like four daughters of a vicar and his wife in a cold vicarage. I read magazines. Moira played games on her laptop. Tracey did sums and drew sketches on a pad with a pencil. And Lizzie kept as quiet as a tongueless mouse as though she wanted to fit in but didn't know how to be endearing.

One laugh came when we all went to the supermarket for the weekly provisions. Tracey was pushing the trolley on the vegetable aisle and as soon as she noticed I'd got my eyes on some giant carrots about three yards ahead, she cut me off with the trolley and steered me in the opposite direction. I grabbed a cucumber and she snatched it from my hand. 'Another day, another time,' she said sergeant-majorly.

If we watched television and it looked like a bit of intimacy was about to be shown on the screen, Tracey would press the remote and turn to another channel. Sex was not only abolished; sex became a taboo subject. Sex means bruises. Sex means favoring one girl over another. Sex is forbidden while ever Lizzie lives here.

Well, there wasn't a great deal of it going on before she came!

I truly believed that this post-battering behavior wouldn't last beyond a few days, but after a few days and then a few more days we settled into some bizarre way of living that only I complained about. I did get to have sensible conversations of a sort with Lizzie when my girls were present. I'd talk about being kind to people, how it is so much nicer to give than to receive (not sexually) and say whatever has happened in the past can't be retrieved or altered, it must stay in the past and the only thing to look forward to is a future of happiness in which folks are equal and everyone is nice with each other. I never asked her about the fire or her uncle. I spoke in a motherly way, as I often do with Moira. Occasionally, I'd kiss her head or stroke her hair, but that's as far as it went.

I'll admit there were kisses all around when the girls took themselves off to bed and left me on the sofa. Several nights I had the urge to beg one of them for a favor. 'Can't I sleep with you tonight?' was often stuck in my throat. I so longed to be screwed but longed also for a show of heavy affection.

Amid this... this prolonged torture, Tracey finalized some kind of deal with Sonny Mabon and Angela regarding their takeover of the MAID MOIRA'S business. Because my brain was polluted with thickening frustration, I paid little heed to details of Tracey's amazing deal. The points that spring to mind include a staggering cash transfer to Tracey's bank account – she furiously attempted to get Moira and me to agree to a share. We refused; it had been Tracey's investment in all the outlets that gave MAID MOIRA'S value, and Tracey's diligence and her relentless observance to hard work. We wouldn't accept a penny, and that was that.

As I understand, Sonny Mabon and Angela are investing a fortune to open branches of MAID MOIRA'S in the Midlands and London. They intend to go up-market, ditching bacon sarnies for croissants, avocado, and poached eggs. They're going back to the maid's dress uniform instead of our two-piece that we found comfortable and sexy. We all retain our jobs and Tracey has an option to choose any position she desires.

However, probably the only bits of news that excited me are that the three of us retain 5% each of the entire business no matter how big it grows, and believe me, growth is expected, and the brilliant news that relates to our café on the precinct which both Sonny and Angela seem to look on as the poor relation in the MAID MOIRA'S conglomerate. Our original MAID MOIRA'S is entirely ours – if the earth is destroyed by an asteroid, if the world's richest man buys the company, our lovely little café won't be included in any future deal. We may continue squirting tomato sauce and biting asses (some chance!) over the freezer. We own the original MAID MOIRA'S lock, stock, and both barrels. The clientele in East Leeds just is not ready for an up-market menu.

To the present

1 In the beginning God created the heavens and the earth. 2 Now the earth was formless and void, and darkness was over the surface of

*the deep. And the Spirit of God was hovering over the surface of the
waters.*

And after that, some wise guys went on to write a whole
Bible so who am I to moan that I'm writing my confessions with
presently nothing to confess. As in ancient times, if nothing has
form, then it's up to individuals to be creative.

When I ask myself how weeks can pass without so much as a
wayward ripple, I'm left stupefied. I've only myself to blame for not
assaulting the postman or turning up at Leeds University with a flag
bearing the words FREE SEX. I've gone along with the girls' wishes,
and Marty is one of them, and fallen into the trap of being a clean-
living boring fart whose skin never sees the light of day.

Well, there are two major reasons why this trend is going to
change: first, confessing I've eaten a bunch of bananas gets no-one's
juices flowing, and second, I'm sick of being an uncooked piece of
meat. I need action, and if the girls aren't ready to roast me then I
must go out hunting. Rosa Saint John's confessions can't remain
dead in the desert. The show must go on!

A quiet morning at the café gives me a chance to have a
sensible conversation with Lizzie, although I wish she'd turn sideways
instead of flashing her gorgeous headlamps under my nose. Tracey,
behind me, is lost in a dream, so I ask Lizzie if she misses her uncle.
She surprises me by saying how wickedly she treated him. 'He's so
docile, he could be a donkey,' she says. 'I could tell him to jump
under a bus, and he would jump under a bus.'

'And Russian men are supposed to treat women badly,' I say.

'He's an exception. I used him. I blamed him for saving me...'

'From the fire?'

Lizzie doesn't respond but gazes at the ceiling. Then I see her
fingers stretching and I know she's about to shock me. She stands

erect and murmurs, 'Sorry that I hurt you. And sorry for disrupting your life.'

I'm stunned. I've spent these past weeks trying to get my nearest and dearest to believe Lizzie is human, and if my phone had been recording, I'd have had the evidence. I stroke her cheek but don't reply. She glances with soft eyes. I smile, flick my hand as if to say nothing matters. I guess if Tracey hadn't been three feet away, I'd have lifted Lizzie onto the counter and got her to show me just how sorry she feels. I turned my head so Tracey couldn't see my face, then purposely stared at Lizzie's tits just to test whether she'd react. 'He'll do anything for me,' Lizzie said.

I whispered barely audibly, 'I wish someone would do anything for me.'

Tracey's ears pricked, 'Did you say something?'

'I wish sometimes, we could do anything,' I said.

'Most things,' said Tracey. And that's about the nearest we've got to mentioning sex in what seems like a thousand years.

Late that same afternoon came another visit from Katy and Marty. They called to participate in the game that I see as a test of twin loyalties. It's blatantly obvious that Katy has banned Marty from the bedroom and she's keen to see how he behaves in my presence. Katy trusts me, but she doesn't trust him, and like Tracey and Moira she's testing physical loyalties as well as loyalties of the heart.

Yes, it's a game. Ban sex, then establish whose heart belongs to whom. All those secure relationships that existed before my beating are broken or fractured. Lizzie's the culprit and responsible for all the disasters in our lives. Katy wishes to know if Marty loves me more than he loves her. Tracey won't allow me to neglect Moira. Moira thought we were immensely happy and doesn't particularly sympathize with my constant yearning for sex. Emotionally Lizzie belongs to no-one, and no-one but me wants her for so much as a kitchen cleaner. As for me, I'm emotionally glued to Tracey, Moira, and Katy, and to some extent, Marty and everyone knows I'd sleep with any of them, even Marty with Katy's permission.

But hearts are powerful motivators, and folks have different priorities; they like to feel stable, need that sense of belonging primarily to one other, and when an intruder such as Lizzie comes along and somehow entangles us in a web of mistrust, their whole world falls apart and they're left feeling insecure and perhaps a tad vengeful.

Oh, I know I shouldn't have brought Lizzie to our bedroom and Marty had no right turning up late evening without Katy's knowledge. Yes, I betrayed my girls by bringing Lizzie here – big deal. But one bizarre sex session hardly merits putting shutters on holes for weeks on end – they're festering, and in the long run that only leads to further decay.

So, Katy watches Marty and everyone watches Lizzie and Moira dips her eyes and Tracey smiles a little falsely and I serve coffees and make the ever so faintest references to sex which nobody hears and nobody responds to. It's a silly game with no winners, and it's been going on for weeks, goddammit!

A call to action

My day off work and by some miracle Tracey has persuaded Moira to go to the café with her and Lizzie for the first time in months. Moira hasn't shared a shift with the headcase since Lizzie gripped her arms in the recess behind the clothes store. Unbelievable.

I'm aware that some folks will find this whole situation unbelievable… six lovers (well, loosely speaking) all abstaining from sex because of one violent encounter between me and Lizzie. But

these kinds of things happen in life – relationships pricked by thorns
get infected, and if they're not treated immediately, the poison
spreads. That's all there is to it. They all need to realize that life's
too short and it's time to bury the hatchet, or more precisely the
fingers, or in Marty's case, the dick.

Before nine, I go to town on the bus with the mad intention
of picking up a stranger, taking him or her to a hotel room, indulging
in a wild sex session, then returning home soon after the girls have
finished at the café. Yes, it's got so bad that I'm prepared to resort to
Tracey's old ways of procuring providers of excitement in the bars
and cafes in town; she's forced me into this with her inane rule of
physical separation. Does she understand my frustration and my
need to gather confessions?

I wander around the market area, talk to a young guy running
a greetings card stall. He seems nice and friendly but just as I think
I'm making progress his wife returns with a handful of shopping bags
– she spotty and has unwashed hair and speaks with a lisp. Failure
one!

I see a few homeless folks who'd love a bed just for sleeping
and get one or two filthy stares from guys who see me glaring at their
bulges. The town appears hostile but I'm not prepared to give up
without trying. And the more I walk, the hornier I become.

On the corner of Briggate, there's a young couple who looks
like swingers. I smile easily, say 'Good morning'. The girl's eyes
sparkle but his face goes as sour as grapefruit and the moment
passes disappointingly.

As I'm pondering which wine bar to visit, I reach the
pavement near the Town Hall and suddenly a flyer is pushed in my
hand by a pretty girl with long blonde hair. I stop, draw back my
head, and say, 'You're cute.' She thanks me as a second equally
attractive girl comes to her side with a handful of flyers. The first girl

points to the flyer and tells me it's advertising a gig. 'I'd do a gig with you two,' I laugh. Then I ask if they're having fun. The second girl says that she's thirsty and I offer to buy them a drink. They thank me again. I point to a bar across the road and they both start giggling. Then the blonde girl pulls the most astonishing amused expression and tells me they're thirteen years old and the other girl says that a coffee would be nice. God, my belly wobbles – if I'd have looked like them at thirteen, I'd have been a mother at fourteen – at thirteen my tits were knots in a piece of string.

I buy them coffees in cardboard cups and a sandwich each from the bakers down a side street, then go on my travels after notching up another failure. I think about going home before I get arrested.

Ten minutes later I'm on Boar Lane and pushing open the glass door of a wine bar. Within two seconds I notice a handsome guy slumped at a table like he's down on his luck. He's smartly dressed and wears stubble on his chin.

I take my wine glass from the bartender then casually glide to the guy's table – there are dozens of other empty seats but I'm taking the one that faces him. 'End of the world?' I say.

He looks up, nods his head. 'I'm thinking,' he says like he wants privacy.

'Me too, I'm always thinking.' He ignores me. I make his glass ping by twanging my fingers.

'You're familiar,' he says referring to my attitude rather than my features.

'Whose bed did you sleep in last night?' I say then start to annoy him by moving his glass around the table. He doesn't bite, keeps his head low, and flattens one hand on the table's surface. He reminds me of a client from the sex club who'd screw me without acknowledging I was a living human.

For half an hour I size him up and behave like a bitch on heat. Surely, he'll get from his seat and drag me by the hair to a back alley and pound my ass at least until two in the afternoon. Then he says, 'You're a good listener.' Jesus – he hasn't spoken!

'I'm good at other things,' I say then dare to place a finger under his chin and raise his head. The last thing I expected was to see his eyes filled with tears, and what ensues is even worse… I sit there for another hour listening to a tale of how his girlfriend left two nights ago and she's gone back to her parents' house; she no longer loves him but he loves her and he can't exist without her. She's amazing, she's beautiful, she's all he ever desired, and now she's gone. Holy shit! Do I need this?

Eventually, I escape after advising the guy to quickly find another girl to play with and to arouse the jealousy in his partner, then I add that I've got an appointment for a job interview – good luck!

That old battle of love versus sex rears its ugly head once more. How many times during the past two years have these human desires clashed head-on in this brutal war? Why folks can't separate the needs of the body from the requirements of the harp-tunes in the heart, I don't know. I love Tracey, Moira, and Katy but give me one last screw in life and I guess I'd choose Lizzie to tango with.

Homecoming

When I enter the room, Moira and Lizzie are relaxed on the sofa and Tracey occupies her usual armchair. I remark jokingly that I've been to town to find 'some dirty bastard' to screw my ass. No comments or shuffling in seats, so I ask who wants a coffee, then proceed to the kitchen with my tail between my legs. I feel like running about the house naked if only to get a reaction.

After delivering the drinks I sit at the kitchen table, prop my jaw on my hands and stare at the opposite wall. I consider my options: getting drunk on gin, amusing myself in the shower, or confronting the girls about this ridiculous way of living. I think about the guy in the wine bar and console myself with the thought that the girls are still here – one or two could have left, just as his girlfriend did.

A couple of minutes pass before Lizzie comes to wash her cup then she too sits at the table. I don't know why, but I say, 'I made you coffee because you like coffee.'

'Sure,' she says as an unconscious response.

'Know what…' I begin, 'when I and Katy were kids, we once went to a graveyard and stole some flowers for our mother. Mother likes flowers so we thought we'd make her happy. We gave her the flowers and she screwed up her face like we'd put a curse on her. 'Lilies are for dead folks,' she said. Then she told us about giving… if ever you feel the generosity to give, consider the person who's receiving the gift. Be sure they're going to receive the gift in the same spirit.'

Lizzie leaned forward a little and whispered, 'Is that aimed at me? I'm sorry, Rosa.'

She knew I was referring to her biting of my ass when I leaned over the freezer and her beating of me with the eighteen-inch-long dildo. Her hand flickered as if she was going to touch me but the open door faced Tracey.

'I love giving,' I say, 'whether it's presents or kisses – seeing folks' eyes light with gratitude, knowing I'm doing some good in the world is so very pleasurable.'

'I'll remember that,' says Lizzie.

I nod toward Moira to ensure Lizzie knows who I'm talking about. 'She's so innocent, so kind. I could cuddle her forever.' Then I nod toward Tracey, 'And she's got a heart of gold – she couldn't hurt anyone.'

Lizzie whispers again. 'Isn't she hurting you now?'

'It's a temporary rebuke, I say. 'We'll all realize soon that we need each other's support, we can't go on forever being physically distant.' Then I flash an enormous smile, and say, 'And when the frigidity ends...'

'It won't end for me,' says Lizzie quietly.

'It will, my girl – the thaw always comes when the sun shines.'

A while after Lizzie returns to her seat on the sofa, Moira joins me at the table. She has no compunction about holding my hand and gazing sweetly into my eyes. 'Did you enjoy your morning of freedom?' she says.

I squeeze her fingers. 'I love you, Moira.'

'I love you too, Mum,' she smiles. 'I haven't forgotten about you.'

We have a wordless conversation, tiny gestures with meanings known only to both of us, and after a few minutes, she too returns to the sofa and immediately unfolds her laptop with contentedness on her face.

A long time passes before Tracey relents and takes two coffee cups to the sink. She pauses behind me, leans over my shoulder, and says, 'You've been on the prowl.'

'Drew a blank,' I say.

At last, she sits next to me, then loops her arm through mine. 'This is for the safety of us all. She could have killed you had it not been for Marty. You're doing a good job by taming her, but I've got to think of Moira.'

'I think of Moira,' I say.

'You, me, and Moira must get through this,' says Tracey. 'If Lizzie changes… well, that's another matter.'

'She needs time and understanding,' I say.

'We'll see,' says Tracey taking my cup and asking if I'd like a glass of gin.

A reevaluation

Sleeping on the sofa in my own house when there are three comfy beds upstairs is bonkers. The same thing happens every night – I feel resentful. I spend half the night thinking about which bed I should invade. I don't imagine that Moira is going to scream if I sneak up the stairs and nestle beneath her duvet with my head between her legs giving her pleasure. She won't yell for Tracey, and she certainly won't yell for Lizzie. And is Lizzie going to shout for the other girls' assistance – no way! There's only Tracey who'd prevent me from having sex. She'd say, 'Let's get this sorted. Let's find unity. We need to feel at ease with each other.'

I am at ease. I don't give a shit what's going on in anyone's mind, I just need a body to play with or a couple of bodies to play with me. Hell, it's insane. I wouldn't mind screwing any of my girls even if afterward they deafened me with curses.

In the dead of night, I crept to the landing and for a few minutes listened to the girls breathing. I got myself excited musing about their warm bodies housing dreams of being screwed. The urge to sneak into Moira's bed proved so powerful that I went into the bathroom and sat on the toilet with my pajama bottoms acting as manacles on my ankles and the pajama top unbuttoned and dropped low on my arms. God, I felt like screaming, 'Wake up, bring the big black dildo, and screw me until morning – carry me to any bed and relieve my suffering.'

After fifteen minutes of finger activity, I heard Tracey get from her bed. I flushed the toilet, then went downstairs before she came out onto the landing. Why the hell didn't I ask her to come to the room for sex, I don't know. She could have said no. She could have said, 'Just this once.'

By 3 a.m. I'm regretting my decision to go to town this morning. Surely, my future doesn't involve picking up waifs and strays who are either underage or another woman's cast-offs. It's amazing how sensible thought is mashed when bodily urges are running rampant. If the guy in the wine bar had pushed me to the floor and split me in half as the few customers and the bartender watched, I'd have been overjoyed. Isn't that disgusting? And my girls are partly to blame.

If I don't have sex in the next day or two, I'm going to bring the sucker machine downstairs, rig myself up to the wires, and lay on the sofa for a whole week with the dial set on 10. I'll make the room stink, I'll have the front window open so neighbors can listen to my moans, I'll have a sign outside on the pavement reading 'FREE ENTRY – come watch the nympho!'

By 4 a.m. I'm assessing the likelihood of finding a chink in Katy and Marty's barricade and wondering if I could call on Katy when her girls are at school and lure her to her shower cubical, or could I phone Marty when he's at work and demand that for old time's sake he takes me to the countryside to show me what rabbits do in the fields. I question Harry and Sally's finances – 'Hey, impecunious young couple, how about I give you a few hundred pounds for a threesome in your cozy bedroom. I don't mind a crying baby if you make the sex last for five or six hours!' Then there are Kev and Timmy on the council estate. Is it feasible to believe I could track down Lucy or Jake? And then I spend a whole hour dwelling on a return to the cages at SMA – oh, all that filthy sex from filthy folks paying for sex – but Sonny Mabon's comment about me being twenty-six a year ago doesn't bode well for me being twenty-seven now. 'Please, Angela, give an old girl another opportunity to experience multiple orgasms. Promise, I won't disappoint the clients!'

The horrible truth is that I haven't the courage to go back to the cages; I'm so afraid of someone telling me that I'm past my best and it's time I wore big white knickers and a thick bra. I never envisaged this cruelty even when Lizzie was beating my body and sinking her teeth into my vital organs. Help me!

Four on a shift

It's never happened before, but with Tracey's reluctance to leave a girl at my mercy, whether at the café or in the house, we found ourselves compacted behind the counter with eight hands available to fry a single egg. Oddly, we were quite talkative and the customers didn't know whose legs to ogle or whose tits got them salivating most. There was a heap of lewd remarks dashing from one end of the café to the other.

Tracey popped out a couple of times in the MAID MOIRA'S van; one swift journey to Headingley and another to collect cans of pop from the wholesalers. There wasn't the usual frostiness between Moira and Lizzie and they both appeared eager to be over-polite. I did get the opportunity to remind Lizzie about one of my most inventive sex acts by holding the water pipe that comes down the wall at the side of the hot plate; I looped a finger around my neck to conjure up the scene when I entangled her in the barbed wire before giving her body its first taste of girl on girl sex. Lizzie looked both pleased and embarrassed before whispering, 'Seems years ago'.

Other than that, nothing significant occurred until about 11.30 when Moira remarked that she intended to dye her hair. She had a desire to be dark-blonde instead of black, and as she's telling her the reasons why she's fed up looking the way she does, Lizzie pipes up that she has several boxes of hair dye in her bedroom drawer at the Glover Street apartment. 'Come to think of it,' she adds, 'there are one or two things that I need from my bedroom.'

I offer to go with her to collect them. Lizzie goes silent before claiming that in her present kindly mood she doesn't wish to see her uncle. She wouldn't know how to handle him because she's so used to bossing him about and being heartless. I suggest I could call at number 37, then maybe visit Katy to ascertain if she and Marty have arrived at a truce. Lizzie ponders, then gets a sandwich bag and starts making a list of items for me to pick up. Tracey asks me to call at the local store on the way home for milk, sprouts, and a jar of coffee. I'm happy to have a little freedom to begin the afternoon – who knows, I may bump into Sally pushing her pram.

An interesting development

When the café closes, the girls jump in the van and Tracey drives off with her hand waving from the open window. I set off for Glover Street intending to call on my sister after I've been. I deliberate on what to say to Katy. Lately, she's not been too forthcoming and a part of her may believe that I'm doing Marty favors without her knowing. I plan to be warm, comforting, and assuring – perhaps she'll cry and I'll lead her upstairs to her shower, seduce her tenderly and tell her that all she needs is sisterly love. God, I can't recall the last time I fondled her and I hope she's missed me as much as I've missed her.

The door at 37 is slightly ajar. I knock, hold the sandwich bag in my hand and it flaps in the sideways breeze. I knock again, wait almost half a minute before Uncle Russia gingerly pulls back the door. His fixed brown eyes inspect me, 'The girl in Lizzie's bed,' he says.

I show him the bag with the list in Lizzie's handwriting. 'She wants these things,' I say.

He bends his neck, invites me in. Seconds later we're standing in the kitchen and he slurps the last spoonful of soup from a bowl before putting the bag close to his nose. I tell him that the items are in her bedroom, at least I think that's where they are. He goes off. I hear her bedroom door open and after not too long he starts grunting as if confused. 'Some things are in her drawers, I believe,' I shout.

He returns with two items, plonks them on the table, then hurries off again with the list held at head-height. Drawers open and close, eventually he brings in five boxes of hair dye. I point out the blonde shades and tell him to return the others. Slowly the items are found but I notice he hasn't found her shoes. I remind him; he grunts some more, then finds Lizzie's shoes on a rack next to the front door. He nods several times as though he's completed a task. He stiffens his hand and says again, 'The girl in Lizzie's bed.'

'Yes,' I say. I watch him get a carrier bag from a cupboard beneath the sink and begin likening him to some old-fashioned butler that serves a demanding master. Then memories of being in Lizzie's bed flood my mind. I recall hammering into her with the strap-on, listening to her erotic cries, watching her juices flow, and feeling immensely proud of my actions, and then she suddenly bangs on the headboard to summon Uncle Russia. She orders him to screw my ass and he obliges just as he's obliging now. Wow! Thrusting and being thrust into. Great memories.

I wonder if I dare… He loads the bag with the items then places the bag at my feet. I cough. He glances as if to ask if he's fulfilled his duties. 'One last thing,' I say nervously.

'I do what Lizzie requests,' he says.

I cough again, breathe deeply. 'Lizzie says you've to screw my ass,' I say not very confidently. There's not a flicker of disobedience on his expression. A surge of bravery sends tingles to my thighs. I take one step toward the table and notice him staring at the bottom of my skirt. I force myself to continue and be bold. I lean forward over the table with my legs parted and my fingers searching to fix on the table's edges. I don't move when I'm in position and my brain is willing him to please me.

I shut my eyes tightly and hope for the best. What have I done? For God's sake, touch me.

There is no communication, just his footsteps on the tiled floor. I feel colder air as he folds my skirt on the dip in my back; he heaves down my knickers quickly then circles the palms of his hands on my ass cheeks. I'm kind of scared and disbelieving what I'll do for sex. He steps closer and I feel his dick hardening as it touches my skin. I part my legs further and pray that he doesn't speak. Then he's inside me, pressing considerately until flesh cushions on flesh. I relax and allow him to screw me at a pace he finds sustainable. His dick is thick, yet unusually cold. It's like being given ice-cream in a scorching summer; those sensations of having something alive inside me clog my throat with thrills, have my belly rippling on the table's surface, and leave me rejoicing that my sexless period has ended. I want to plead with him to screw me harder but accept his gift with untold enthusiasm. I meet each thrust with gratitude and wet his entry with approval. And just as in Lizzie's purple-painted bedroom his rhythm is constant and he doesn't pause or complain. I think of days gone by when sex came so plentifully and many times unappreciated. He slides in me like he is meant to be there; like he's responding to dreams as a figment of my imagination; it's as though he knew I were coming here and is prepared to give of his best.

And it ends abruptly and Uncle Russia retreats like his job is done. I stand, reach down to reposition my knickers. I see his dick is erect and he's fumbling to shove it inside his pants. I argue with myself for three seconds then mount the table, lay on my back, and kick off my knickers. 'A little bit more,' I say and my wish is granted. He fills my pussy and I orgasm almost immediately.

How many weirder sex acts than this? He dawdles toward the bag and holds it at my belly. Crazily, I look in the bag and say, 'Well, that's everything for now.' I retrieve my knickers, view the scene of my triumph, then leave 37 Glover Street without uttering another word.

Smiling

I return home no later than expected with the groceries and Lizzie's items, needless to say, that I didn't visit Katy – I'll save her shower for another day. The relief to my body proves amazing; it feels like I've lost my virginity and I'm ready to lose it another twenty times in the next twenty hours.

The girls are flitting about the house without any real purpose; Moira is collecting laundry and keeps rushing to and fro to fill the washing machine and Lizzie is fiddling with the hoover as if it's gone on strike and doesn't wish to cooperate with her. Tracey, as ever is performing a multitude of tasks and has hardly noticed I'm here. I make us all a coffee and shout 'tea-break' but no-one pays attention so I go to the sofa with a handful of biscuits.

The thrill of being screwed wears off quickly, much quicker than expected. I get to thinking how ridiculous it is being so close to inaccessible bodies. I used to have similar thoughts over Marty's body when we'd stop speaking for a day or two, but this has gone on for weeks. Throughout the world, households are filled with folks who sustain petty grievances; husbands and wives who form bubbles of stubbornness around unhappy faces and prolong the agony of separation well beyond what is sensible. Is this sensible? No sex because a girl with a sensational body sets fire to her parents' home when she was six or seven years old? No sex because Tracey thinks I'm neglecting Moira? No sex because... Because what – sexlessness is the latest craze and even Rosa Saint John is expected to follow.

'There are coffees on the kitchen table,' I yell. 'If you can't do anything else with your asses, sit on them!'

One by one they grab their coffee cups and sit in the room. Lizzie thanks me for getting her items and passes Moira the boxes of hair dye. Tracey makes a comment that hints Moira will be a new attraction with blonde hair. Does it make a difference – the pain of resistance will worsen as I'm banned from molesting her. All of a sudden, I juxtapose an image of four friends sitting in a room with the present scene, and my brain cries that we're supposed to be lovers and if what Tracey intimates is true that Moira will be a new attraction, then we should be carrying her to the sink, dying her hair, and as soon as it changes color ravishing her body until well past midnight.

We've become four friends with no-go areas. But when I gaze at Lizzie in the far armchair and see her want-to-please face I think how far she has come in a few short weeks; that bolshiness has gone, that air of 'I'm important' has gone. If she'd come with me to

Uncle Russia's place, I doubt she'd have had the temerity to request a length of dick (that's if she ever did). She's no threat to anyone yet she still owns that irresistible body that houses ten tons of pleasure. It's insane to uphold these distinct unconnected sleeping areas. Chatting about soap powder, Brussel sprouts or a new bag for the hoover isn't what four hot-blooded girls should find interesting topics. Can't one of the girls be honest and declare a throbbing desire to have her pussy violated? Won't any one of the girls stand, strip off and beg to be taken lecherously?

They talk, I observe. I ask myself if any girl has fantasized about the four of us being in bed – it's never happened. The most Tracey and Moira have seen of Lizzie's firm tits are the two fabulous arcs in the neckline of her uniform. I often dream of Lizzie and Moira flat on their backs with me and Tracey hovering over them. We could pass hours in rapturous harmony, swapping, repositioning, spitting out orgasms like they're pips from oranges. We could stay in bed from last shift on Saturday until Monday morning, screwing as never in our lives, living on nectar, riding sensations like they're waves on the oceans, and using our energies for a communal purpose.

Instead, 'The kitchen floor needs mopping,' says Tracey.

'I'll do it,' says Lizzie.

In the pause that follows I want to say, 'Well, I'll take Moira to her bedroom and chew her until she's dry.'

Moira smiles and tells us she's going to play on her laptop. Perhaps I should have told Uncle Russia that he'd been ordered to screw me without a break for at least the next six weeks.

Attack mode

I know it's easy to over-use a single word but I feel triply neglected. Uncle Russia provided temporary relief, but I need a real fix, and my girls have gone off to their bedrooms leaving three kisses on my floundering skin. Three pleading looks didn't unbutton their pajamas. I opened my mouth to suck in their scent. My last memory is their footsteps on the stair carpet and the landing light being extinguished. Another eight-hour shift on the sofa with a pillow and blanket.

If love is a beach and neglect is the tide, steadily, erosion occurs. My love for Tracey and Moira is getting washed in saltwater. When the tide goes out it takes with it a few more grains of sand. Don't they know how much I ache to be touched and replenished with warmth?

If I were to compare the kisses, then Lizzie's kiss lasted the longest. Lizzie's lips swept mine, kind of apologetically, kind of acknowledging my punishment, as if she were saying, 'It's all my fault – if I hadn't arrived here, you're bodies would be entangled in lust. I'll go to my bed and imagine myself in my necklace of barbed wire and what you once did to me.'

There's got to be a weak link, and I know of my three girls, my sister and Marty, the weakest link is Marty. If I called him at work and said I am desperate for sex, he'd oblige me. But would I stoop so low and risk hurting my sister?

It's 10.45 and I twirl my phone in my fingers, even consider texting Moira or Lizzie. 'Sneak downstairs in the middle of the night – let me love you on the sofa. I promise you a stream of sensations and I'll muffle your cries with my hand so Tracey doesn't hear you.' Oh God, just to touch one of them, to see her mouth contort with pleasure.

I hold the phone to face me, text, 'Want to talk?'

Ten seconds later the phone buzzes. 'Rosa…'

'Hi, sis… I'm missing you.'

There's a very long pause. 'That night with Lizzie… did Marty know Lizzie was there?'

'No.'

'Did he think you were alone?'

'I only told you that Tracey and Moira were going to London – no-one else.'

'How did Marty know?'

'You must have told him.'

'Did I?'

"You must have done. He wouldn't have called if the girls were here.'

'So why did he call?'

'To see me I guess.'

'What for? Did he ask you to sleep with him?'

'No.'

'Did you ask him to sleep with you?'

'No, Katy. I had no idea he was coming.'

'Why did he?'

'I don't know.'

'You must have an idea.'

'Sometime before he'd mentioned he felt guilty about you working so many hours. He admitted he didn't feel worthy of being a father to your girls. Maybe he needed someone to talk to… someone he thinks understands him.'

'I don't trust him, Rosa.'

'Does that mean that you don't trust me?'

She didn't reply instantly, then she said not too convincingly, 'Of course, I trust you.'

'When folks don't trust each other, they end up sleeping on the sofa.'

She giggles quietly. 'That's where I am now.'

'Me too… I've been here weeks. There's not only you who's got suspicions. To Tracey and Moira, I'm a leper. They won't come near me – I'm dangerous to know.'

'You won't like that,' says Katy.

'Frustrated… is that what you mean. God, I'm dying…'

'They don't let you…'

'Nothing… not a sniff.'

'How long's it been?'

'Since that night.'

'Are you at the café in the morning?' she says.

'Day off.'

'Call on me, around 10.'

'Okay, sis. Hope the sofa is comfy.'

A shaky alliance

When the girls disturb my sleep in the morning, I try to be cheerful and crack a couple of jokes about them being naughty on the freezer in the café's rear area. They ignore me; I get offered a coffee. Tracey says the room has a sweaty smell and she'll bring home a stock of air-fresheners. Only Moira smiles at me. I feel like an intruder who's been allowed to doss on the sofa for a single night. They leave; the most I get is a wave, again from Moira.

Minutes later a sense of liberation imbues my body. I feel like a teenager whose parents have left her alone in their home while they've gone out in the car and she's desperate to see her flesh, eager to exhibit herself to mirrors and do things she loves doing in private. I take the coffee cup to the kitchen and before the dregs have swilled down the plughole, I'm naked and sitting cross-legged in the middle of the table. I'm not short of ideas on what to do but am aware that Katy may be on the menu in two hours hence.

Then I stand at the kitchen window for a minute before rushing to the hall and opening the front door to let fresh air dance on my skin. If old folks in the bungalows opposite are peeping, well, they'll get a reminder of their glorious pasts. I don't care. I'd like to run into the street and dare pedestrians to screw me on the road. I'd like to be bold, doing something completely outrageous would shock the girls into paying me attention.

As soon as I shut the door, I run to the shower. Another minute and my body is smothered in soap and the joy of being free is causing giddiness. I relieve myself of frustration, lay on the shower basin, and let the water cascade on my thighs, then soaked and dripping I skip to my bedroom window and stand so close to the glass that steam clouds the pane. I turn, parade before the mirrors, exercise lewdly just to be outlandish. I go to Moira's bedroom and lay on her bed then go to Lizzie's bed and sniff her pillow. I lean over the landing railing and remember Marty hammering my ass after he'd bound me to the struts with cable-ties. God, I'm tempted to bypass Katy's and use Tracey's full collection of sex toys all in one delightful morning. And then, to be nuts, I crawl head-first down the stairs letting my tits twang over each edge of each carpeted step. I feel fantastic, run to the kitchen, and abuse the vegetables in the refrigerator while sitting on a chair with my feet balanced on the table's rim. When we're eating our dinner, I'll secretly smile knowing I've got closer to the girls than they realize.

Oh, I do more than this. I view the short film of Lizzie playing with herself on Moira's bed from the evening she beat me. I return to the shower with a dildo – use your imagination – and make full use of the hour from 8.30 t 9.30. Then I get to wondering why Katy asked me how long it's been since I've had sex.

I dress sexily in a short skirt and a tiny top. I check for evidence I've been indulging myself in the girls' bedrooms; wet footprints will dry, I spray scent in the air, then come downstairs hoping Katy is feeling generous and will take pity on her younger sister by… (?)

Everyone who knows Katy understands that she's far from impulsive. She's methodical, slow to warm up. I guess like many eldest sisters, likes to take charge, and do things in an orderly manner. But the second I shut her front door, she takes my hand and leads me up the stairs to her capacious landing. She's wearing one of those expressions that says, 'Don't speak, don't argue, I'm not only going to do you a favor but take a favor from you.' She's taller than me and can be dominant when she desires. She puts her hands on my waist then sort of scoops my top like she's undressing one of her daughters when she was four years old. I must say, I'm tingling fabulously and urging her to be more adventurous than on the few previous occasions we've been naughty. 'Rosa…'

'What?' I murmur.

'This is going to be memorable,'

Now, I'm sorry to disappoint, but some folks will know just what I'm not prepared to reveal in my confessions, and of all my encounters the ones between me and Katy are the only ones that remain largely secret. We showered together… so what! We enjoyed sharing pleasure… so what! But I'm never going to give detailed descriptions of going too far with my sister – even Rosa Saint John has limits.

In Lizzie's parlance, Katy scored 9 out of ten. She put a smile on my face, but when we came downstairs to her kitchen, Katy didn't gleam with satisfaction. She stood with her arms folded leaning against the work surface and immediately addressed the subject of me sleeping on the sofa. 'Is there not more to it?' she says suspiciously.

'More to what?'

'More than rough sex with Lizzie… Tracey and Moira should know you by now.'

'They do know me.'

'Then why are they persecuting you?'

'The rot's set in – just as with you and Marty. I guess the trust has gone.'

Katy tightens the arm-fold. 'I'll speak to them.'

'You don't have to.'

'I want to,' she says.

I don't argue. I think perhaps Katy can be a mediator and make my girls realize they've created an issue over nothing. Lizzie isn't going to burn us alive in our beds – well, those who have a bed, anyway.

Two days – no progress

Shifts in the cafe with Tracey and Moira, then Tracey and Lizzie are about as eventful as watching the clouds. Where once there'd have been touching behind the counter and suggestions of what we may do when we get home, it's now references to how Sonny and Angela are getting on expanding the business or counting the packs of bacon or discussing the pros and cons of cleaning brands. Why don't the girls just cook me on the hotplate and serve me on a large plate to hungry customers? I'll taste delicious coated in tomato sauce.

I think back to the days after Marty left and dreamed about having sex on tap; someone living with me with a sexual appetite, someone to satiate my needs. And now I've three girls and they're all behaving like novice nuns. It's so ironic that I gave up working the cages to be emotionally and physically attached to Tracey and Moira, and it seems we're as far apart as ever. I feel like screaming and announcing to the guys sitting at the tables that it's got so bad I've had to resort to cavorting with my sister again and tell lies to a Russian guy whose name I don't know so he'll give me a little pounding on his fucking kitchen table.

At home, it's no better. The girls have started locking the bathroom door when they're in the shower. They've probably put iron bars around their beds, threaded with live electric cables, even planted explosive mines in their bedroom doorways, fixed chastity belts over their privates just in case I'm clever enough the surmount the obstacles. I'm forgetting the shape of their tits and believing that the next time I see a pussy it will look like Caroline's hedgehog – remember Caroline, the fat cow who was Marty's office boss who he brought to my house for a threesome? Good grief, I'm desperate enough to have a threesome with residents from a care home.

Question for Tracey, Moira, and Lizzie... 'Do you know what screwing is?' And they'd reply, 'Sure, it's something you do with a screwdriver – turning a screw.'

They taste their dinner, lick their fingers when opening paper bags, poke peas down the plughole, suck milk through straws from a glass, strip covers off cushions, rub cloths when cleaning, but none of these verbs are used on my body. All I get are kisses before they go to bed. I'd get more action being locked up in a women's prison.

There's been one event that could have turned into a major event but it proved dismally disappointing. I saw Sally again not too far from the local shop, of course, pushing the baby in the damned perambulator and practicing motherhood by uttering 'coo' and 'there-there' every second stride. She looked quite fit; her coat was open and her belly was flatter than weeks ago. And her tits weren't bursting with gallons of milk. And her bare legs were inviting.

I thought I'd go in for the kill and kissed her on the lips in broad daylight. I'd make it obvious that sex is on the agenda, with mothers, fathers, absolutely anyone! I couldn't wait to ask her if Harry's hours at work had returned to normal, or is he still financially embarrassed (and the embarrassment extends to her too)? Hopes soared when she claimed Harry is in danger of redundancy. 'Tell Harry I'll pay him two hundred quid for ten sessions on the tower block roof.' I didn't say that. I offered to assist her if things got difficult. I weaved into sentences oblique references to sex. 'It would be nice to get together.' 'I've missed our little meetings.' 'Nice to see you looking fit.' 'We used to have so much fun.'

God, why didn't I just say that Sally tasted like one of those trifles that has the mouth salivating even before a spoonful is delivered? Why didn't I offer her a bundle of banknotes for unfettered access to her slightly stretched body? Harry can work my shifts at the café while I suck on her milk glands snug in her bed while the baby plays with its pacifier in the cot.

Her parents are supporting her!

What's wrong with folk? Has a Bill been passed in parliament outlawing sexual contact? The best I got was the promise of a walk in summer or perhaps a picnic in the park. It's not inside sandwiches where I'd prefer to stick a cucumber, but Sally doesn't understand my predicament.

Katy the diplomat

Katy had Marty drop her off outside the house at about 8 p.m. on Saturday. She looked smart and business-like in her two-piece black suit with dark red lipstick and she smelled of perfume with a peachy odor. She entered the room with an air of confidence, as though we were students and she'd come to advise us on our coursework.

I hadn't warned the girls about the visit. Tracey glanced at me instantly as if to ask what I'm up to. Lizzie and Moira were relaxed and greeted Katy with affable smiles. I made five coffees. The silence in the room was uncomfortable. When we were all seated and gazing at the carpet, we heard the rain start to lash on the window. Miraculously, the rain ceased inside a minute, and Katy and I said simultaneously, 'That was strange.' There were murmurs of laughter from all but Tracey.

Katy sat forward in the armchair and tucked her knees neatly into a bent-legged pose. She glanced at each of us, then said sharply, 'Let's not beat about the bush. It's gone horribly wrong for all of us.'

Moira nodded. She knew what Katy meant.

Lizzie scratched the top of her left tit and swung her ponytail over her shoulder.

Tracey, who nowadays appears gentile, suddenly acquired one of those faces she wore in her whoring days. 'Who says it's gone horribly wrong? What's gone horribly wrong?'

'I've got eyes,' said Katy. 'The atmosphere here is not what it used to be.'

'Is that aimed at me?' said Lizzie straightening her back.

Katy raised her palms. 'Girls, we'll get nowhere pretending.'

'What have I done to you?' asked Lizzie.

I held out my hands, 'Hey, she's only come here to try and get us talking.'

'We talk,' said Tracey bluntly.

'Not like we used to do,' admitted Moira.

'And it's all my fault,' said Lizzie.

'This isn't about individuals,' said Katy defensively, 'it's about us all. Goodness, we've been like frozen statues since that evening.'

'There you go,' said Lizzie. 'Have you come here to tell me to leave?' Then Lizzie stared at the rest of us. 'Is this what it's all about – get big sister to come to kick me out? I'm a danger. I've gone in the head.'

'Don't be stupid,' I said.

'It's not like that,' said Moira.

'It's about sex,' said Katy. 'None of us, not you girls, me or Marty are having sex anymore.'

'You're just like your sister,' said Tracey nastily. 'Everything revolves around sex.'

I poked my finger in Tracey's direction. 'Hey, cool it, Katy isn't like me.'

'She's worse,' said Lizzie.

'Stop the arguing,' pleaded Moira.

'This is getting out of hand,' I said, 'I just thought we may be able to talk, tell each other how we feel, resolve our issues, get back to being kind and loving.'

'Get back to having sex three times a day,' said Tracey sarcastically. God, how she hates anyone interfering in our relationship. This wasn't Tracey – this was Tracey in crocodile mode.

'I wish we'd all understand each other's problems,' said Katy.

'What problems have you got?' asked Tracey.

'I see my sister unhappy. I see cracks appearing in my relationship with Marty.'

'Why? Because he came here that night?' said Tracey.

'Don't blame Marty,' I said.

'No, blame me,' yelled Lizzie, 'I beat you, not him.'

'Did he know you were here?' said Katy.

Lizzie sprang to her feet, snarled, 'You fucking bitch,' and lunged toward Katy. Katy grabbed her wrists and let Lizzie struggle as she towered over her. I jumped up, eased Lizzie back to her seat, and heard Tracey's curses bounce in my ears and Moira's cries for calm go unheeded. Everyone was shouting. Katy insisted that Marty came for a reason and one of us must know why.

'We were in London – me and Moira were in London, you stupid cow,' said Tracey.

'He probably came to see me – I've told you,' I implored Katy.

'He's got his nose up her ass!' shouted Lizzie for badness.

'He hasn't,' Moira said. 'Rosa wouldn't' do that.'

'Rosa would have any nose up her ass,' said Katy.

I stood square on to her. 'I can't believe you have said that...'

Tracey laughed, 'There are so many noses up Rosa's ass that no-one can breathe.'

'I was trying to get the noses out when I flogged her,' said Lizzie.

'Please... please...' begged Moira who stands and starts praying to Jesus. 'We must not argue. We're making everything worse.'

'She started it,' said Lizzie pointing at Katy.

'You wouldn't thank me if I commented on you and Marty,' said Tracey to Katy.

'Can't we sit down and talk calmly?' I yelled.

'Let's have a fucking orgy to please Rosa,' said Tracey.

I tried to be calm and allay Tracey's fears, she sounded jealous, though jealous of what, I didn't know. I attempted to cuddled her but she shrugged me off and slumped on the sofa with her arms crossed. Moira patted her knee. Lizzie was seething and looked ready to storm out of the house. Katy flung her arms in the air and declared that she'd wasted her time. She'd only tried to help. 'What thanks do I get?' she said.

There were more chunters, petty insults and unkind words before Katy slammed the front door on the way out.

Lizzie said she'd leave. She could see that she isn't wanted.

'You're wanted,' I told her.

'Stay,' said Moira.

'This is a right fuck-up,' said Tracey.

'I just long for all of you,' I said. 'I miss your affection. I miss touching all of you. I can't go on like this.'

'Can we sort something out,' said Moira simply.

'Other than an orgy, there's nothing to sort out,' said Tracey.

I ran upstairs, got my jacket, and put on a pair of shoes, came down and screamed at the girls, 'I'm going to find a big dick, okay?' Then off I went up the street probably hoping that either Lizzie or Moira would chase after me.

Every two or three yards I looked over my shoulder but no-one followed me. I'm dispensable, too demanding, and they're not going to miss me if I jump into the river and sink to the bottom. I felt so low and wanted to die.

Where now?

The initial explosion, which has the one who flees vowing never to return, seldom lasts more than a few minutes. Before I traverse 300 yards and I realize the girls aren't coming to haul me back to the house, I want to go back and curse them, threaten that I'll go to the other side of town and become a streetwalker, or do it with anyone for free because I'm addicted to sex. Anger surges and I think I've been treated unfairly. Tracey shouldn't have been so hostile toward Katy, not that Katy proved tactful or understanding.

I march on, reach the precinct, and dip in my pockets for keys. I soon learn that this jacket has been hanging unused for quite a few months and the only item in the pockets is Joe's business card. I can't sulk inside the café nor return home to a locked door in the dead of night. I hadn't brought my phone, so calling Joe is impossible.

I got to wondering about Joe, a guy who appreciated my body along with his mates. Remember him? He was one of the 16 or 17 guys that had the pleasure of me in the barroom at SMA when Tracey held the post of Recruitment Manager. I became his favorite girl, and when I left the cages, he organized a gang-bang at a hotel in town and in the space of 11 hours I earned close to three grand. Joe wanted to set me up in an apartment, maybe take me on holiday, so he and his mates would own a plaything. At least, that's how I remember it. I could have become a kept-woman, living in luxury with half my time spent on my back.

Maybe some day soon, I'll call Joe and ask him if I'm still on the menu.

I think of walking to the riverbank and sleeping on a bough, ten feet up a tree so the wildlife can't nibble my toes. What reception will I get if I call at Katy's house? 'Stuff your bitches up your ass – and keep them away from Marty!' It's almost dark and I'm homeless – should I go beg Sally to consent to a threesome with her and Harry? Two hundred quid for one night of energetic sex and Sally can pause to feed the baby while Harry continues solo.

Pathetically, I wander toward the street where Katy lives a few doors down from Sally, but I don't have the guts to hammer on either door or plead for comfort. I do a full lap of local streets, pass my parents' house without being tempted to call, and before I know it, I'm back at the precinct and again searching my pockets, only to discover that Joe's card remains the only occupant.

I pass the recess where Lizzie tried to grope Moira and suddenly find myself finding excuses to call on Uncle Russia. 'Lizzie says you didn't leave bruises on my ass.' 'Lizzie says you didn't fulfill my needs.' 'Lizzie's giving you a second chance to make amends.'

I gulp, tell myself to stop masticating meaty thoughts, and head to Glover Street with a bold tongue and a buzz in my knickers. Uncle Russia can only slam the door in my face and tell me to piss off.

The inner light glows through the window. I stand on the opposite pavement, building courage and preparing an opening line, then proceed with determination to secure shelter from the night that gets colder.

I knock twice, and unlike before, the uncle responds quickly. He stares at me like I'm a total stranger, with not a blink, not a fractional movement of his head. 'Is Lizzie here?' I ask. He doesn't flinch. 'Lizzie... has she arrived?'

'No,' he says bluntly.

'She told me to call,' I say. I immediately sense that he doesn't believe me. The door closes ever so slightly and I fear being rejected. I expel a nervous laugh, push out one knee, and shift my jacket back on my shoulders, then smile like a flirt. 'Do you want to make the most of my body – I've nothing better to do.'

He considers my proposal but doesn't hurry. And after ten seconds or so says, 'Where is Lizzie?'

'My house,' I say. 'By now she'll be wrapped up in bed.'

He moves to the side, allows me to enter. He glances at my bare legs and makes an animalistic noise. 'Sex...' he says, 'you've come here for sex.'

'As much sex as you're willing to give,' I say boldly. 'I'm a hungry girl.'

He doesn't look at me but leads me to a white painted door decorated with a crucifix. He opens the door and wafts his hand telling me to enter. I see his bedroom and I'm quite astonished; it's immaculate, mostly white with religious ornaments on drawer tops and walls. Then he retreats for a minute and I hear the curtains being drawn in the room and a key turning in the front door lock. When he comes back his stern expression has gone. He still refuses to look at me but tugs on his shirt as if it's an order for me to undress.

God, now I do feel like a prostitute, a mobile hooker visiting a client. He watches me as I strip and I notice his eyes dart to my tits when I take off my bra. He breathes out as if he's seen the most glorious sight in his life. He points to the bed and I lay in the center with my legs open. It's so clinical as if I'm about to have an internal examination by a doctor.

Uncle Russia takes off his pants but leaves on his shirt. He shuffles on his knees to a position between my thighs, then he presses against my body, jerks a couple of times, and keeps on staring at my tits – they excite him and I begin to wonder if he's ever seen a girls' breasts in his life. As he becomes erect, he jerks again, purposely making my tits bounce. Not once does his eyes divert as he eases into me, not with force but ensuring I'm wet enough to receive him. And that customary rhythm begins, straight up, straight down, occasionally thrusting a tad harder to get my tits moving. Most guys watch the entry point but Uncle Russia seems obsessed with the shape of my breasts and he'd love to sink his mouth over my nipples but for some reason desists.

I've stopped thinking about the girls and feel mildly amused that his thick dick isn't thrilling me. Such a bizarre situation has me recalling the punters at SMA who I didn't delight in having sex with. Uncle Russia's sex is like exercise, like no-one ever taught him about passion or being utterly disgusting. I'd let him screw me upside down, gobble my pussy until I squirted all over his face, but he just keeps on pumping methodically as if he doesn't know about orgasms or even ejaculation. And it goes on for perhaps fifteen minutes before he cups his hands to his mouth to say that he needs a drink. He leaves me sprawled on the bed and I instinctively start fingering myself. I've barely warmed up and I ponder whether I should give him instructions.

Almost ten minutes pass before he returns with what I presume is a glass of vodka. He sips from the glass, places the glass on the drawer top, then begins round two with his eyes again fixed on my tits. I take his wrist and guide his hand over my belly. His eyes become like headlamps as I settle his right hand on my tit. Jesus, momentarily he stops screwing me. He can't believe what a tit feels like and I feel his dick get harder in my pussy. I tell him he can fondle me. I tell him that I have no objection to anything he wants to do. I won't be shocked. 'Fuck me, however...' I say just to get his pistons working fruitfully. And he feels my tits with both hands and his mouth opens like he's thinking about sucking my nipples; I urge him to become adventurous but I've to settle for a slight increase in rhythm and a thicker warmer dick.

I lift my hips, do the best I can to counter his thrusts with mine. I'm stretching my knees to both sides of the room and yelling in my head for him to screw me brutally. But he doesn't. He again stops, leaves the bedroom, and leaves me gagging to be screwed by the big black dildo we keep in the wardrobe at home.

Time passes. I get to thinking he's fallen asleep. I shout 'hello' twice. I finger myself repeatedly and half-determine to have an orgasm if it's the last thing I do in this bed. I even imagine that Lizzie's going to turn up and go ballistic with her uncle before forcing him to hold me as she beats me to death with an unknown

implement. If I die, it's Tracey and Moira's fault, and maybe Katy's –
frankly, I don't care so long as there is a heap of pleasure attached to
dying.

'Screw me with all you've got,' I say when he eventually
returns to the bedroom. He sits on the bed close to my shoulders. I
think he's going to grab my head and force his dick into my mouth.
'Do anything,' I say. Then he leans over, squeezes a breast in each
hand, and gloats as my nipples pop in and out of the gaps between
his fingers. I notice his dick starts to stand like a telegraph pole. I
talk dirty to him, encourage him to use his imagination and do to me
all the things he's ever yearned to do with a woman's body. And
when he's got maximum satisfaction from squeezing my tits and his
dick can't grow any bigger, he rolls me over, puts me in the doggy
position, and begins screwing my ass with a vigor not previously
exhibited. I moan and beg for punishment. I call him 'big boy', tell
him to give me the full length of his dick, I say I can last all night, 'You
can screw me till morning comes, I'll take everything, I'm a filthy
bitch with an insatiable appetite for sex.' And just as I'm reaching the
pleasure zone and believing Uncle Russia is stepping through the
gears... yes, you've guessed it... he stops again, goes over to the
drawers, and empties his glass of vodka down his throat. He goes to
the front room to fill his glass and I hear the vodka gurgling from the
bottle. Inside I'm screaming for his return – don't let the sensations
perish – 'For fuck's sake, split me in half!'

He comes back and pulls me off the bed, shoves me flat
against the wall. I'm urging him to poke me viciously; I part my legs
and dip my eyes like I'm telling him what to do. He lifts my arms, lays
them on the surface of the wall and tells me to keep them there.
Excitement rises – go down on me, impale me, just batter my body
with lust... and he glares at my tits like they're the most magnificent
objects on the face of the earth, slowly starts to fondle me before

finding the courage to suck on my nipples ever so gently and then runs his tongue over their tips. Oh sure, I can't complain but I wish he knew better how to satisfy a woman. I let him do as he wishes but for many minutes, I'm feeling frustrated. When he takes a breath, I snatch the collar of his shirt and push him away from me. He looks confused though he doesn't resist. I push him onto the bed, lift his shirt to his belly, then get astride his body and slowly sink on his penis. It's apparent he's venturing into new territory – he's unsure what to do. I glide up and down, shift angles, ride his dick like it's one of those dildos that a girl suckers to the floor. And all the while he keeps his eyes on my tits and revels as they bounce above him. I purposely keep stooping forward, tormenting him, reclining, and asking him how much he wants to suck my tits. 'You're not moving,' I say, 'not until my first orgasm.'

And as I'm teasing him by dipping my nipples repeatedly in his mouth the first orgasm spills on his body. I demand more, keep on pounding him until beads of sweat form on his forehead. It's probably the longest session so far and I hope to sustain it until daylight arrives. I even think he's going to ejaculate inside me, and I utter all the dirty phrases I can think of. Hell, and then he struggles free and rolls off the bed. He points at my tits and says, 'Beautiful, so very beautiful.'

And the night wore on; many more glasses of vodka, taking me from the front and behind and always with an obsessive desire to feel my tits or stare at them and make them bounce. We screwed not too adventurously but by the time he could no longer sustain an erection, I'd at least stained his pure white bedsheets with my juices. I'd given the poor guy a brief education in the art of screwing. At around three in the morning, I left him asleep in his chair in the room. Perhaps if I'd had cash on me, I'd have left a tip. Maybe next time if there is a next time. Maybe next time I'll teach him what a guy can do with his tongue.

A sticky welcome

What's peculiar to me but alien to most folks I know is that after sex I'm usually horny; I used to come home after a night in the cages and let myself loose on my own body. I dawdle home thinking that a few hours in the garden shed will temper my urges – the front door is sure to be locked and I'm not getting blamed for disturbing the girls' sleep. I creep the final few yards to the front of my house and surprisingly see a dim light bleaching the curtains; it's the room lamp that is seldom illuminated.

Quietly, I press down the door handle. The door opens and I imagine that Tracey and Lizzie are waiting, weaponized with the eighteen-inch dildo and a metal torture rod. I sneak inside, close the door and peep into the room through the gap between the door and its frame. Moira is asleep on the sofa. My heart sinks – she waited for me.

I tip-toe to her side, sit on an exposed part of a cushion and touch her hair. She wakes, hazily, whispers 'Mum'.

'My sweet little maid,' I say.

'I couldn't go to bed knowing you weren't here.'

'I love you, girl. You are so beautiful.'

'I've been frightened,' she murmurs. 'What if…'

'What if the ghosts of the night got me?' I whisper.

She snuggles her head on my tits and purses her lips to be kissed. As I kiss her, I run my fingers across her scalp and tell her I'll never leave her. Wherever I go, she goes, until death, we shall never part. It's an intimate moment; for weeks we've not been alone and

I've almost forgotten what a thrill it gives me to touch her. She's warm, so sweetly submissive in her partial slumber and her lips are parted and receptive. I kiss her again and lick the inside of her mouth. Our tongues touch and I turn her shoulder so her body is facing the ceiling, and as she lays almost flat, I notice the top button of her pajamas is unfastened and briefly glimpse the curve of her tiny tits. With our lips a fraction apart I say softly, 'I want you, Moira, I've craved for you so very much. I can't exist another hour...'

'Without touching me,' finishes Moira.

She gazes into my eyes as I undo more buttons on her pajama top and I understand Uncle Russia's fascination with my tits. Moira sighs and moves her arms to the sides of her body, and when I caress her it is the most wonderful moment of recent times. I feel that I'm wanted and all the despair in my heart seeps from my body.

I slacken her pajama bottoms and slide my hand over her shaven mound. She props one leg on my knees and widens her eyes as I please her. 'One day, Moira, I'll bring so much joy to your body that your world will change and you'll become like me. There'll be no turning back, forever we'll swoon in sensations and nothing or no-one will come between us.'

'I love you, Rosa,' she stutters, and she says Rosa over and over knowing how much she turns me on. I make love to her in the dull hush-hush light of our silent room where at last a breakthrough is dawning.

Strange Sunday

After sending Moira back to her bed and having a few hours of sleep on the sofa, I showered and dressed in my old rags before the girls arose late in the morning. Tracey was the first to come downstairs and she glanced quite seriously at me and said, 'Well...'

I flashed a smile and told her that yesterday was yesterday – the past isn't something to carry to the future. She made me a coffee and grudgingly agreed that arguing is something we're not used to. She'd felt aggrieved by Katy's insinuation that somehow one of us was to blame for Marty's behavior, and that simply isn't how it is.

I suppose I spoke defensively about Marty. He isn't the type of guy to cause trouble. Katy doesn't know him as I know him, and yes, I admitted that Marty's biggest problem is letting go of me and accepting that he belongs to my sister.

Tracey's not dumb; she knows that the reason he came to our house on that fateful evening was to have sex with me. And if Lizzie hadn't been there, who knows what may have happened. Tracey isn't possessive; she's been sex-motivated, she knows the score, and she isn't particularly concerned if I sleep with Marty, Katy, or both of them at the same time. Tracey needs to trust me and be able to believe whatever I tell her, and she needs to be sure that our relationship is solid and not endangered by these young girls I can't stop ogling. Moira isn't included, but Lizzie is.

I assure Tracey that I don't love Lizzie. Just before Lizzie and Moira join us, I'm trying to convince Tracey she should have a dabble of Lizzie's body – if she went there once, she'd realize the true nature of Lizzie's assets. 'You've never seen the girl naked,' I said, 'God, she's spectacular and tastes of the finest quality honey. Screw Lizzie once and you'll be there every day.'

The suggestion lightened the mood though not sufficient for us to embrace or offer to get the other on the kitchen table and have something different for breakfast. Lizzie and Moira immediately noticed that we were talking and relief spread on their faces.

But I've got to say, after these opening expressions of honesty, we soon returned to interacting like we've done lately at the café. We cleaned, did the laundry, prepared dinner, and went about the house like we were workers and not four girls keen to rip off each other's knickers and bind ankles to the west and east of any fixture.

Mid-afternoon, I did get the chance to show Tracey what I meant by Lizzie's gorgeous body. We were changing the curtains in our bedroom when we saw Lizzie flash by our bedroom door and go to the bathroom. We heard water fall on the shower basin, then we heard Lizzie curse. I beckoned Tracey to come and nosy not too far from the doorway. Lizzie suddenly saunters from the bathroom to her bedroom on the opposite side of the landing. I don't think she knew we were upstairs. She's naked and making Tracey's eyes bulge like they haven't in at least a year. And when Lizzie strolls back, she stops outside our door and unknowingly gives Tracey a full-frontal view of her delights before going into the bathroom and shutting the door. 'Wouldn't you mind a chunk of that?' I whisper to Tracey.

Tracey holds her tits as if to ask, 'What kind of tits has she got?' Then she points to her pussy and shoves out her tongue. 'God, she's perfect, ever so neat, ever so...'

'Scrumptious"' I suggest.

The moment passes but I hope Tracey has seen Lizzie in a new light. I just wish she'd believe that housing a headcase is worth it if the compensations outweigh the dangers.

Many times, I attempted to create a sexual theme to exchanges of words. I'd talk about beds, limbs, exercising, holes, blue tits nesting in the garden, 'coming to the shop', ask for a drink of juice, and spurt out sexual innuendoes like rainfall, but no-one was biting and no-one offered to take me upstairs and perform the necessary invasion of my body. Only Moira would have willingly pleased me but the weeks-long detachment remained in force.

By Sunday evening I'm in one of those moods where I truly think that it's been twenty or thirty years since I last had sex. Oh, the regulars do their round in my head, so too the new addition of Uncle Russia. But I yearn for comfortable sex, in the familiar surrounds of the room or a girl's bedroom; I'd just like a couple of hours jam-packed with thrills and maybe two or three thunderous orgasms. As my desires grow stronger, I forget about the warfare and the abandonment of physical contact and escape to the shower to dream-up a way to shock the girls into submission. Surely, if I can get Tracey to cave in, they'll all cave in. It takes only one genius move to return the house to its normal way of living.

So, there I am knee-deep in soap bubbles and plotting to blindfold and handcuff myself and then throw my body on the carpet between the sofa and the armchairs in the hope the girls will pounce on me to express their eternal forgiveness. Yes, a gag too, and maybe something appropriate dangling between my legs. Maybe I'll write 'SCREW ME NOW' in gold paint on my belly. Maybe I could draw arrows pointing to entry points. I'm not asking for the earth.

Then I think of the superb dress Tracey presented for my birthday back in March. It's sexy without being over-the-top. I could style my hair, wear scarlet lipstick, and patent leather high-heeled shoes. Who could resist? And scanty pink underwear beneath, and perfume dabbed on my neck.

I go for the kill, spend almost an hour preparing my flesh for suction and violation. They can have me one at a time or three at a time and render me unfit for a shift at the café in the morning. I don't care, just please have sex with me.

Confidence is high as I step sideways down the stairs – it would be a disaster toppling off a step in my high-heels. I hear the girls talking, take a deep breath when I reach the room door, push it open then parade in like a supermodel on a catwalk. Their heads turn – promising. I go straight to the kitchen, pour myself a full glass of gin, then return to stand in front of the sofa facing Moira – Lizzie to the left of me, Tracey to the right of me. I take a sip from the glass. 'You look so beautiful,' says Moira.

'The girl is on heat,' says Tracey.

'That's the hottest I've seen her,' says Lizzie. 'You look sophisticated.'

'Not sexy,' I say.

'You look wonderful,' says Moira. 'You're not going out, are you?'

'Here with my girls, for the whole evening,' I say.

Tracey leans toward me and lifts the hem of the dress. 'Jesus, she's wearing knickers.'

Lizzie makes a terrible joke. 'Well, she doesn't want sex.'

'Oh,' says Moira innocently.

To be shameless, I gulp the full glass of gin, then return to the kitchen for a refill. I stand again at the fireside, burp, then ask anyone if they'd like to tango.

They're winding me up, especially Tracey and Lizzie whose postures don't change and whose eyes don't signal hunger. I start sipping at the second glass. I realize my plan didn't extend far enough. I think Moira pities me; if she had the courage she'd rise from the sofa and wrap her legs around my waist and maybe plant a huge love-bite on my neck, taste the perfume and scream 'I'll screw you.'

I sip again. Tracey tells me not to spill gin on the dress. I face her, lift the dress over my head, and lay it neatly on her lap.

'High heels and underwear,' says Lizzie.

'They suit you,' says Moira referring to the heels.

What do I do now – take off my bra and pants, drop to my knees and plead for sex? I keep sipping the gin. I feel awkward, kind of stupid: this is the worst kind of rejection, it's humiliating and I can think of nothing to say.

About a minute passes before Tracey collects the dress in her hand then collects me with the other hand. She leads me to the stairs, turns to pull a face at Moira and Lizzie. She takes me to our bedroom, sits me on the bed. 'Hey, girl, don't embarrass yourself. Give it time, there's a lot gone on and it won't get back to how it was by you being impatient.'

She puts her arm on my shoulders. 'I hate it like this,' I say.

'We all do,' says Tracey. 'Something will happen to break the ice. Be strong. Let's all wait for the right moment to come along.'

Mitigating circumstances

It's not as if I haven't stretched myself to atone for the crime of bringing Lizzie to live with us. I don't record all the hours I spend giving motherly counsel to the girl with the former fetish for beating her sex partners. Little chats here and there, occasional visits to her bedroom, fully-clothed, nose to nose dialogues at the kitchen table, all are efforts to redeem Lizzie's pent up anger and to ensure she proceeds through life without haughty self-confidence and a total disregard for others' feelings.

I rarely, if ever, get commended. Sure, if I were not sticking to Tracey's rule of temporary celibacy and groping Lizzie's ass or tweaking her nipples at every opportunity, I'd be condemned. Tracey and Moira could accuse me of stoking the fire if I were igniting Lizzie's flame every two minutes, and no doubt they would, but they don't go about shouting that I've done a wonderful job and they can tell that Lizzie is mellowing with each day that passes.

Lizzie hasn't skinned a cat or left teeth marks in tits or buttocks. There are many times she's placid, polite, and eager to please. I could say she's an asset to the MAID MOIRA'S team or a grand addition to the cleaning team in our home. I could say that she doesn't invade Tracey or Moira's bedroom and she's never once tried to gobble me in my sofa sleeps (shucks!). I could say all kinds of things that exemplify Lizzie's progress – it's down to me – but it's just accepted like it's happened magically and I don't deserve any credit.

Folks keep distances between them long after the reason for coldness dissipates. I can't help thinking that Katy, Marty, Tracey, Lizzie, and Moira should be shaken up in a mighty big bag until their clothes have disintegrated and their limbs are so intertwined that it'll take them a year to separate. In my opinion, the best way to deal with negative feelings is to do something positively erotic – if I had some method of doing it, I bind and gag the lot of them, put them in a line, and give each a few hours of bodily abuse until 'Hallelujah' became a constant chorus.

Monday's surprise

When Moira stayed at home on Monday morning and Tracey said that she had phone calls to make and would arrive at the café later, I seriously considered approaching Lizzie to ask if she fancied having a secret rendezvous to have sex. I didn't know where we could go or how we could find excuses to get away from prying eyes, but her body had suddenly become available – at least my eyes would be let loose for an hour or two and my mind would go into overdrive.

Before we unlocked the shutter, I'd got two plans in my head. She could sneak downstairs to the sofa in the middle of the night or once again claim she needed to collect items from Uncle Russia's, and she dare not go on her own. Lizzie was in a good mood and she even made a comment that suggested she is tired of the restrictions. 'Tracey sometimes overplays things,' she said.

I told her that Tracey needs a pack of sausages up her ass, and Lizzie laughed.

But from the turning of the sign on the café door, we were flooded with customers and barely got a chance to discuss more than a customer's order or whether we had sufficient stock to cope with the rush. We took money, we served breakfasts and takeaways, cleaned the tables and floor, and swapped a few looks that wondered when trade was going to slow. There came a moment of amusement when we were both stood near the freezer in the rear of the café; Lizzie grinned and referred to our first physical contact – when she bit my ass as I leaned over the freezer looking for the door keys. Lizzie pushed on her teeth with a finger, said pointing to a front seating area, 'Shall we ask for a five-minute break?'

I grabbed the water pipe and stuck out my tongue, 'Two hours would be better.' And we knew what each other meant – the desire for sex was rising and by the look in Lizzie's eyes she was telling me I could have her body if something could be arranged.

Then half an hour later, behind the counter, I put my hand under Lizzie's skirt and held it there on her leg joint. I'm sure she felt a little horny; she pushed back her shoulders and twisted her frame so I got a clear view of her tits. 'I want you,' I whispered, and Lizzie nodded, not obviously, but she certainly nodded.

When Tracey appeared about 10.30, we went back to being good girls who'd lost the keys to their chastity belts. When Lizzie went to clear a table, I'd tell Tracey she was missing out. I brought up the fact that Tracey's eyes lit up when she saw Lizzie naked the other day. Lizzie could rejuvenate her interest in sex. Let's end this crazy abstinence and get back to proper living. Tracey made up an excuse of being distracted by the MAID MOIRA'S takeover by Sonny and Angela. I said folks keep on screwing even when they work 12-hour shifts. I got nowhere. I got nowhere but didn't desist making sexual innuendoes until we shut shop at just after 12.30.

And then...

Boiling desire

We climbed in the MAID MOIRA'S van and Tracey drove us home. I remember us passing the health clinic and thinking of that time I saw Sally coming out of the gateway with her baby. I thought too whether Lizzie is serious about us having sex. By the time we stopped outside the house, I was kind of resigned to spending another boring afternoon and evening being superficially friendly while still wearing knickers and bras and not coming within a mile of an orgasm.

We got out of the van, seemed to hang about on the pavement before the front door opened. And then... it happened.

There in the doorway appeared a fantastically gorgeous young woman with long blonde freshly straightened hair. Her lips looked thicker. She wore a brown dress looped around her neck; bare shoulders that somehow looked wider, fuller. Those tiny tits were snug on her chest and her slender body hinged backward as she raised her chin and gazed at the sky. 'Is it going to rain?' asked Moira.

'Hey, girl, what have you done?' asked Tracey.

'Beautiful,' remarked Lizzie.

I just stared. Astonished... yes. Lost in wonderment... yes.
But God, if there is such a thing as instant desire to screw someone in
the next second exists, then that's what happened to me. My entire
body bubbled with liquid lust. I fixed my eyes on Moira's neck under
her chin and don't know how I stopped myself from ravishing her.

She said, 'I've dyed my hair, straightened my curls – this is
the dress I bought a while ago.' Then she glanced at Tracey and
asked if she'd take her to the computer store to buy a new game for
her laptop. They all went into the house and I'm left erupting in my
knickers truly believing this has to be the most amazing sight in my
life. The little sweet virgin maid who I love dearly is now the sexiest
female in the Solar System – and she wants to go to a computer
store... with Tracey... in a van!

I stumbled into the hall, saw Moira from behind. It was as if
I'd left her as a child this morning and returned to find her a woman.
She turned. I had my mouth open and my arms were trembling. I
found the strength to touch one shoulder and say, 'I'm so proud of
you.'

'Do I look okay?' she said.

I pecked her lips as weird sensations sprung from a hundred
different sources. 'I whispered, 'You are the most beautiful girl I've
ever seen. I love you.'

'And I love you, Rosa,' she said. She called me Rosa. Oh,
death, come and collect me at the height of happiness!

But what followed is almost as startling as seeing Moira
transformed. Tracey didn't take off her coat, she merely swung the
van keys on a finger and asked Moira if she'd enough money to buy
the game she wanted. Tracey stepped closer to the doorway and I
gasped, 'You're leaving,' like I couldn't bear to be distracted from
Moira's appearance.

'We'll only be half an hour,' said Tracey. The computer store is on the far side of the precinct. Lizzie echoed the 'half an hour.'

Before I knew it, Tracey and Moira were disappearing onto the street and I'm glancing at Lizzie like I'm in a state of shock. The door closes. Lizzie goes to the window to watch the girls get in the van. I hear the van drive off. Lizzie snatches my arm and tugs me toward the kitchen. She leans against the work surface and parts her legs. Our eyes meet and it's clear what's about to happen. I stand slightly to her side in a similar pose. We don't say another word but guide our hands into each other's knickers. Like promiscuous schoolgirls hiding in a cupboard on a corridor, we begin poking each other as if we've got minutes to reach an orgasm; both of us are wet from the start, both of us are eager to please and to be pleased, both of us are using our wrists as if we're performing some mad ritual that needs to be completed inside the fastest possible time.

We puff and blow and balance on the balls of our feet. There are dirty kisses and most pressing of all desperate urges to rip off our clothes – but we can't take our clothes off. Forceful pokes, three fingers and four fingers, races to stolen satisfaction as our bodies jerk and welcome the invasions. Faster Lizzie. Harder Rosa. They'll be back soon. One more minute. Two more minutes. Oh God, screw me. Let's do it again tomorrow. I want more than this! So do I. So do I. Oh God, I'm about to... Do it! Do it!

Open the window. Wash our hands. Make a coffee. That was super. Have we time to do it again. Yes. No. Just another two minutes. Oh God, that was fabulous. We giggle, spray the air freshener. Lizzie rushes upstairs to change. I smell my fingers. I wish that had been Moira. Is Moira going to play on her laptop when she returns?

It can't last

Moira doesn't spend the remainder of the day on her laptop; she floats about the house, as do all of us. I can't keep my eyes off her. I can't stop thinking not only how much I desire her but how much I love her. This ridiculous imposition of sexual restraint can't last; my patience and tolerance to Tracey's barbaric rule are crumbling. We must get back to the life we had. I am going to possess Moira's body before the end of the week even if it means falling out with Tracey.

At every opportunity, I seek to make mischief. I tell Lizzie that Tracey and I were in our bedroom when she paused at the doorway on her way to the shower. I tell Lizzie that Tracey drooled over her body. I lie and say that Tracey's sexual urges stirred for the first time in ages and Tracey admitted to me that she has vowed to give Lizzie the benefit of her expertise.

I tell Tracey that Lizzie questions me about how good she is in bed. I tell her too that I've seen Lizzie clandestinely gazing at her legs when she's reposed in the armchair. 'There's no doubt in my mind that Lizzie would love to screw you.' Tracey sort of smirked and her eyes said she isn't averse to the idea.

And multiple times I whisper to Moira that we're going to be together before the end of the week. I don't care if I cause a rift with the other girls; I'll sacrifice anything for her.

Things are going on in each girl's head. I see occasional touches, displays of affection that weren't common even a week ago. This past day or two bathrobes have been worn during the day; oh sure, the robes are closed with fastened belts and underwear beneath but it's a sign that the chill is in its dying days.

I do know that since seeing Moira my belly is like a stormy ocean. Lizzie's attention soothed me for a while but watching Moira when she walks by or watching her relax by my side on the sofa is undiluted agony. I've told her I love her a thousand times. I keep uttering, 'You are beautiful,' and each time she says, 'Thanks, Rosa,' not 'Thanks, Mum,' the words bring about powerful urges to accost her in the very next second. I can't recall wanting sex with someone so badly. It's a unique desire to screw her until the last tick of life.

Moira tells me not to worry. I don't know what that means. She says she understands how I feel and my suffering isn't going to continue. Not only has her appearance changed, but she seems more mature and it crosses my mind that she's preparing a surprise – one that will benefit all of us.

The day did end eventually. The girls went to bed and I went to the kitchen table to entertain myself.

Unfathomable developments

I know something is brewing when Tracey and I head for the café and leave the girls alone in the house. This has never happened; in the past, Tracey wouldn't trust Lizzie to keep her hands off Moira and I sense her attitude is softening. If I had to guess, she's mellowed since seeing Lizzie naked and at last, is seeking to repair the fractures that have kept us from each other's beds. Mark my words, sooner or later Tracey is going to make a play for the girl with the super-long ponytail and the tits as firm as rubber humps.

During the first couple of hours, Tracey is fairly quiet even though I make a few jokes about me having heard her creep into Lizzie's bed in the dead of night. I tell her I've even seen Lizzie's hair dangling on the room window when she's been screwing her on the bedroom window ledge. I say that the rain on the windowpanes the previous night was Lizzie having an orgasm. I say they've put cracks in the room ceiling by bouncing so hard on Lizzie's bed.

Tracey looks nonplussed. She'll admit that one day she may be tempted to go a few rounds with Lizzie, but presently, she's much more to think about. I keep pressing the sex angle and politely inform her that I'm getting tired of suppressing my sexual desires – there's no point in four girls sharing the same house if they're not sharing the same bed.

As usual, Tracey begs me to be patient. 'It's going to end,' she declares. I tell her quite sternly that if it doesn't end soon, I'll be sleepwalking to Moira's bedroom and devouring Moira's somnolent body in some very wicked dreams.

When the orders slow and we get a chance to lean on the counter with a coffee, I see Tracey's expression become more loving. Then it changes from loving to sad. She looks like she's about to cry. I nudge her, say, 'What's wrong, girl?'

She blinks to block the tears then taps my hand like she's my grandmother. 'You know how much I love you. I don't need to tell you… you know that I do.'

I squeeze her, laugh a little, pretend that I can hold off having sex for another few hours if necessary. 'Maybe I shouldn't have moved in Lizzie the way I did. I pitied her. She was a young girl in need of help.'

Tracey smiles as if to say I'm so lovely for the way I misread situations. She loves it when occasionally I become that old Rosa Naivety Saint John the girl she fingered on the lane behind the church. 'This is nothing to do with Lizzie or Moira. This is to do with you and me.'

'You and me?' I say in surprise.

'You and me… you're the most important person in my life – there's no-one comes close.'

'Me too,' I say.

Tracey smiles again. 'Hey, I'm not stupid. You've at least two loves in your life, and maybe I'm second to Moira.'

'I love both of you.'

'I don't mind that, but I've only got you.'

'And you'll always have me,' I say.

'Will I?' says Tracey.

'I get the impression you're leading me somewhere.'

Tracey goes silent. I reassure her with kisses and cuddles even though there are four guys in the café. She takes a deep breath then suddenly spits out the reason for this strange conversation. 'Sonny Mabon wants me in London.'

Jesus, my face alters. I stand erect. 'He does, does he?'

'As it stands,' begins Tracey, 'what we do with this MAID MOIRA'S is our business. It's the original MAID MOIRA'S and it's not going to change. The Headingley café and the city café are in the hands of Angela – so too those proposed in Sheffield and Wakefield. But Sonny has big plans. He butters me up by telling me I've got enormous potential. He wants me to oversee the preparations for the London sites. He thinks I have an eye for detail and his one objection is to what is on our menu. He wants me to learn about southerners' eating habits. Wants me to do lots of things before the sites open for business.'

'And what have you said?'

'I keep telling him that I can't leave Leeds, and every time I turn down an offer he comes up with another offer, more money, an apartment, transport – what he's offering is insane. He used to praise me when I was the Recruitment Manager at SMA, but not like he praises me now.'

I'm wounded, not because I wish to prevent Tracey from fulfilling her dreams, but because some guy's trying to steal her. 'Is this for good – forever?' I say.

'He said a month or two, then three months, now he says it's for as long as I like. The offer is open-ended. I can't bear the thought of losing you.'

"I'm going nowhere,' I say.

'And that's the point – I'll be there, you'll be here, you'll forget me, I'll become irrelevant. When I return, you'll have a houseful of girls and I'll be nothing more than a reminder of your past.'

God, I get kind of angry – oh yes, I'm a sex-maniac, oh yes, I'm madly in love with Moira and have great hopes of practicing my skills on Lizzie's delicious body for a good while yet, but to toss Tracey aside is inconceivable. Tracey has made me what I am now. Tracey introduced me to sex. Tracey is a masterful performer and even now my talent doesn't compare with hers. 'Don't you fucking dare say that! You and I are for life girl. You impaled me on the lane and you're never going to remove me from your fingertips. I'm Moira's lover and Moira's Mum and I love her like my heart is bleeding love, but you are my other half. If you go away for a month or two, I'll fucking hate you but your place in my bed will never be taken by another. For fucking better or worse, and so long as you don't ask me to bung up my holes, I'll take the worst and break my heart in your absence, and when you return, I'll expect everything – you'll need to screw Moira and me ten times a day until the end of time.'

'I haven't said that I'll go.'

'If you do go. I'll kill you if you don't come back. Promise me you will.'

Tracey's eyes dribbled tears. 'If I do accept his offer, three months maximum, and I'll be back with more money than we've ever dreamed of.'

'I don't give a shit about money. It's you and Moira I want, bare-assed and penniless, or dressed in pink stockings and a suspender belt.'

I haven't to mention anything to the girls. Tracey will continue her negotiations with Sonny Mabon and she'll keep me informed at every new twist. By noon, I didn't know what to think. However, what I do know, is that when I fall in love, my love is for life, and I'll never stop loving Tracey.

More developments

To sit on the sofa with a glass of gin in my hand is normally a sign that I'm high with hopes of success with one of my girls. The truth is one mood replaces another every five seconds. I get a glimpse of Moira with her sexy blonde hair wearing a different dress I bought her from the clothes store next to the precinct. She brings tingles to sensitive parts of my body – she's about as gorgeous as gorgeous can be and the desire to undress her is supercharged. Then I'm sulking, reliving those months when Tracey and I lost touch and thinking what kind of a future I'll have if my heart is shrunk by 50%. I rely on Tracey for my sanity, and so much else. Then I notice Lizzie walking about in her bathrobe with an open front. I recall screwing her in the café after I'd handcuffed her to the water pipe. Different sensations, purely sexual, ride up my legs. Please, Tracey, don't leave me. Oh God, Moira, why are you so deliciously beautiful. I want sex. I don't want sex. I want peace of mind. I want things to be normal. I want the four of us to go to bed and screw eternally.

When Moira passes or sits for a minute to chat, I gawp at her, say things that aren't in tune with my facial expression. 'I can't believe it, you're a woman,' I blurt with my face stained with the potential loss of Tracey.

Moira stares in confusion. She probably thinks I've lost my marbles. I don't so much touch her because I know my hands will be unable to release her. 'I can't believe it, you're a woman,' I repeat as I tilt my head and force tears to roll back into my eyes. 'You are so beautiful, I love you.'

And she says, 'I love you, Rosa.' She loves me, Rosa. She doesn't mention Mum.

'Is anyone wanting to use the shower?' asks Lizzie. Hell, I vision water cascading on Lizzie's tits. I watch Tracey come from the kitchen with a cup of coffee in her hand. As Tracey nears Lizzie, I say without thinking to Lizzie, 'Kiss Tracey on the lips. Kiss her for me.' And so casually, as though it's happened a million times, Tracey allows Lizzie to kiss her lips and responds with a little pressure of her own.

'Satisfied?' says Tracey.

I strain my neck and place my head on the backrest of the sofa, pout my lips for Lizzie to kiss, then she kisses me too. Then I gaze at Moira like I want to swim in the pools of love that are the whites of her eyes. Tracey sits beside me and taps the top of my thigh.

'I suppose it's silly,' she says.

'Everything is silly.'

Moira plays with her hair then asks what's silly.

Tracey blows Moira a kiss, then says, 'Hey, there's not only Rosa who remembers you from SMA – I do. The plain little girl in a black & white maid's outfit. Afraid to speak, tip-toeing up and down the stairway, serving the girls, being so polite and humble.'

'With her tiny tits hidden behind a pinafore,' says Lizzie jokingly. This has gone to be Lizzie's first-ever reference to Moira's body. And then she stuns me and Tracey by saying sincerely, 'Moira, you're stunning. Honestly... stunning.'

I laugh, tell Lizzie that Moira is mine, 'She isn't sharing the shower with you.' Lizzie pretends to be upset and scurries up the stairs. Then for some daft reason, Tracey gets Moira and me to stand for a group hug. It's the closest the three of us have been for many weeks. I think about begging Tracey to tell Sonny Mabon to stick his job offer up his ass. Let's go to bed, screw all afternoon and if needs be, tie each other to the bed so none of us can ever escape.

Sadness mixed with love. Sadness coagulating with desire, stirred by a big spoon in Love's hand. I'm in pain and it shows on my face. I'm in love and it's crunching my heart. I hug Tracey and Moira as if the end of the world is imminent.

And then comes probably the best few minutes we've shared since Lizzie came to live here. A cheeky look sweeps over Tracey's face; her eyes search out the hallway and then she points mischievously at the stairs. She sneaks between me and Moira, walks with her back arched like a soldier on a battlefield and we're instructed to follow her, up the stairs, quietly, avoiding the creaky sides and to the landing. She gets on her belly and crawls to the bathroom doorway and pushes the door a little further open. We follow suit, and moments later we're all staring at Lizzie with her back toward us, in the shower, with her hands gliding up and down her fabulous body. Lizzie is enjoying the touch of the soap; she moves about and isn't aware. Eventually, she washes her thighs, then parts her legs further to lather her pussy in suds. Simultaneously, we yell, 'Woo!' And Lizzie turns sharply. For a second she's unsure how to react. At last, she smiles, opens the cubical door, and poses full-frontal, letting us glory in the sight, letting us holler remarks that we've never said in Lizzie's presence. 'Make the soap vanish,' I say. 'Let me get you a dildo,' says Tracey.

And Moira points to Lizzie's breasts and tells her they're magnificent. Oh, we're having so much fun and smashing down barricades that have dogged us for so very long. I feel sure something is going to develop – I pray that Lizzie will spring from the shower and invite us to share her on my double bed. Moira's face is thick with wonderment. Tracey is drooling like she hasn't drooled for months. I get to my feet thinking I should make the first move, perhaps take off my clothes and encourage the girls to do likewise. And then…

'Is anyone home?' comes a cry from the hall.

'Katy!' I shout as three pairs of eyes peer down the stairs from varying heights.

'Can I talk to all of you?' she asks meekly.

'A minute,' I say. Katy goes into the room. Tracey's expression is quizzical. Moira shrugs her shoulders. Lizzie steps from the shower and looks vaguely disappointed as though she too was expecting the fast to be shattered by group sex.

Katy waits patiently for us to gather before acknowledging us in turn with a tiny nod. She places her hands in prayer, then says meaningfully, 'I've come to apologize. I'm so sorry that I tried to blame any one of you for my suspicions concerning Marty. None of you is to blame. I've been foolish, and I beg your forgiveness.'

Hell, initially we didn't care about an apology – we'd almost climbed the mountain and she'd shunted us to the valley below. The four of us swapped woeful glances – what could have been? what if? – couldn't Katy have chosen a different moment?

She didn't apologize once but more like fifty times in succession. Her relationship with Marty is under stress; there are all kinds of reasons, niggling problems that are nothing but in total amount to something. 'How Lizzie could have anything to do with it, I don't know,' she said. 'I lost all sense of reason. And to think you,

Rosa would encourage Marty, is downright unacceptable. I've been a horrible bitch. I've been rotten to all of you.'

Oddly, Moira came out with the remark, 'So, you and Marty still aren't…?' Moira meant screwing each other, but she didn't finish the sentence.

Katy confessed to sleeping on the sofa. She feels like a lodger in her own house. Marty keeps on creeping, even buying her small gifts, but she just can't come round to signing a peace treaty.

And we listened, and Katy talked, and Katy talked some more and apologized some more during three rounds of coffee and twenty chimes that the row of last week did not affect our relationships. Attempting to relieve Katy from her suffering I explained we'd been watching Lizzie in the shower when she called. We were about to haul her to a bedroom and replace the soap bubbles with froth. Our tongues were hanging as low as our navels and we're getting on amazingly – all we need to rid ourselves of our period of abstinence is one prolonged orgy that ends in utter exhaustion. And what did Katy do? She went on apologizing, letting us know about petty arguments with Marty, what Marty says about this and that, how Marty won't admit that he'd secretly been lusting after one of us, or all of us – she doesn't know.

Multiple times during her repentant outburst, I felt like suggesting that we take Katy upstairs and stab her with dildos until she's vanquished her sins. She wouldn't be so hung up about Marty with the big black dildo rammed up her ass. For God's sake, Katy, when he was mine, he used to take little blue pills just to become the size of a medium sausage.

Moira repeatedly sympathized with Katy, 'When you're used to having sex, it must be difficult to go without,' she said. And added, 'Poor love.'

Tracey consoled her by saying her deprivation will end; all things end eventually. And by the look in Lizzie's eyes, she simply couldn't compute Katy's point of view. She wished Katy luck, if it was needed, then went upstairs soon to be followed by Tracey.

A late afternoon that began so promisingly turned into a long, long evening, and when she departed at gone nine, I and Moira were left stultified side by side on the sofa and thinking we'd done a full shift as marriage guidance counselors. Moira kissed me several times before going to bed and for once, I found it easy to accept that no-one was in the mood for sex. My ears were ringing and crazily I longed for an aspirin.

Wrong, wrong, wrong

I'd have wagered every penny I own – the cash in drawers, boxes, piggy banks, jars, and my bank account – that in the next days, we'd be screwing at least six hours a day in splendid athleticism, in twos, threes, and fours, from the top of the wardrobe to the bottom of the stairs in the hall. I'd have bet on 50-100 orgasms, 50+ showers, and 5,000 decibels of moans. I'd have bet on nakedness more than clothed. I'd have bet on stinking bodies, aching limbs, sex for the sake of sex, and the springs of at least one mattress being broken.

I'd even counted on someone calling the fire brigade to untangle our bodies because we'd all got so sticky that we'd welded into one mass of grossly indecent flesh.

If Katy hadn't called, it's 99% certain that we'd have eaten Lizzie on my bed. I took two aspirins but didn't expect the effect to be more days of no-group-therapy. And I can't put my finger on what happened – it happened. Wednesday, Thursday, and Friday became orgy-free zones.

The last thing the girls and I dreamed of was a second visit from Katy with Marty in tow. There were more apologies and for half the time they were here I kept reiterating the reason I thought Marty came on that fateful evening – he hated Katy working long hours and his opinion of himself as a surrogate father was dismal; Marty felt guilty and needed a friend to console him – I was that friend, no more than that!

We girls told them to bury their grievances. Boldly, Moira asked them if they'd had sex. She seemed interested, and I couldn't think of a reason why.

Anyhow, their presence ruined another evening when we should have been chasing each other around the rooms of the house. Instead, the most pleasure I got was from a glass of gin and a bar of chocolate gifted to me by Moira.

These three days brought more phone calls from Sonny Mabon and Angela; it seemed to me they were exerting endless pressure on Tracey to go to London. I'd tell her she'd be lonely. I'd emphasize the girls' disinterest in money. 'We'd sooner possess your body than your bank balance.' These business folks don't have compassion and all they think of is getting richer and showing how successful they are. Sure, even the likes of Lizzie, Moira, and I can appreciate that Tracey is a whizz at making money but her slim little body is a greater asset than a calculating machine in her head. Without telling me the whole truth, Tracey said she hadn't decided about the future; she wanted my assurance that I'd be there no matter what. Secretly, I hoped both Sonny and Angela would piss off and leave my joint number one love alone.

And I'm ashamed to reveal that one afternoon after a shift at the café with Tracey and Lizzie I made up an excuse to go for a walk; to clear my head, I was suffering the effects of Katy's apologies. But honestly... my thighs were aching to be parted. Some guy in the café had made a disgusting remark about my ass; the guy was deadly serious and wanted me to go with him to his wagon to show me his 'double-barreled shotgun' – he thought I was the sexiest girl in Leeds. So, I had a walk… I went to Glover Street and knocked on the door of number 37 with the hope that Uncle Russia would snatch my hair, drag me to his kitchen table, rip off my knickers, then deliver 500 solid thrusts as my legs trembled in my shoes. I knocked again; Uncle Russia didn't answer the door, maybe he was out shopping for a blow-up doll.

As a result of this failure, I spend several hours musing about Joe, the guy whose business card remained in my jacket pocket. After all this time I wondered how I'd feel getting gang-banged again. Would Joe and his mates be up for it? Would I need to seek the girls' permission to put myself forward for such a delight? I craved sex, and my girls weren't providing me with enough attention.

Not only was I wrong about sex exploding from the faintest brush of skin, but I also misjudged the girls' hunger for it to begin immediately and communally. I had thought, as when Lizzie posed in the shower, one act would lead to unrelenting debauchery that may have seen the shutters remain on the café façade for a day or two.

However, brief forays occurred, and I'm pretty sure of that. Several times I noticed Tracey swap glances with Lizzie; they were those inquiring glances that asked, 'Did you like that?' or 'You want more, don't you?' I'm almost certain that Tracey had visited Lizzie's bedroom in the dead of night and sampled her body. That glint in Tracey's eyes spoke of the good old days when even her teeth were hot. But I couldn't go accusing Tracey of being deceitful because I too had nibbled Lizzie on two shifts at the café; oh, these weren't passionate encounters, more fondles, slipping my hand down her pants, or her letting me kiss her neck in the back room. They were sorties, like desserts before a meal that never arrived. And I believe

Tracey's sorties with Lizzie induced a pang of guilt for one night I woke on the sofa and she's hunched between my legs adding substance to my dreams. I said nothing when I became aware of her, but merely combed her hair with my fingers and showed my appreciation with long low moans that encouraged her to make it last.

As for Moira, well she became a kind of teaser. She'd allow me to kiss her but as soon as my hands wandered or I asked for an invite to her duvet, she'd look lovingly in my eyes and promise me that my days of unfulfillment were limited. 'I promise you they will end. I love you so very much,' she'd say. I know Moira realized what I was going through; she'd press her hand on my pussy and tell me she could feel the frustration. She'd apologize for changing her appearance too soon (whatever that meant) and console me every time I pleaded to touch her. 'I want to see you orgasm with your blonde hair,' I'd say. 'You will, soon, soon, soon.' When is soon? Neither Tracey nor Lizzie attempted to touch Moira, and that is a fact! Moira showed kindness to the girls, but she didn't impose on their territory.

The last observation of this puzzling period came when I popped my head in Moira's bedroom, once more suggesting an hour of adventure. She was sitting on her bed with a large sheet of paper sprawled across a pile of magazines and appearing to design fancy letters with a pack of crayons. The word 'Simple' had been completed.

'Is this a message for me?' I asked.

She giggled, covered the paper with her arms. 'You'll find out soon enough. Go away...'

'God, you're fucking gorgeous,' I said, 'you're wasting your talents – there's so much more that you can do.'

'I know,' she said, 'and I shall.'

Cracking up

By Saturday morning I'm half-convinced that every person I know is conspiring in a plot to deprive me of rampant fulfilling sex for the rest of my life. Yes, even my parents are conspirators! Sally and Harry too! Uncle Russia has been persuaded to bolt his door. Katy and Marty's roles are to fill me with guilt. Tracey and Lizzie are tormentors, agitators, annoyers – the cruel duo! Moira teases me, shuns me, uses me as if I'm a yoyo. I'm cracking up and seriously believing this is never going to end.

Last night, if a burglar had passed the front window, I'd have dragged his stealthy body through the letterbox and ripped off his striped shirt and mask before he could say, 'Give me your money.' I'd have pinned him on the kitchen table and screwed him until the wooden legs buckled under pressure. Yes, then I'd have waited for another burglar, or hoped for the postman to call early. Last night was as frustrating as a night can be without company. At some time today, Joe is receiving a phone call – a discounted gang-bang is in the offing.

If readers could see Moira (new Moira) in her MAID MOIRA'S uniform, they'd understand. Surely, all folks have experienced a sexual urge that's like the biggest wave in the ocean. Moira is indescribable; she's causing impulses in my body to turn into a block of dynamite. Someone's going to learn that Mount 'Rosa' Everest is a living volcano!

Lizzie stays home and we three begin a shift at the café. My mind whirls and goes off on crazy thoughts, and even as we're lifting the shutters, I recommend bringing them down behind us and tying Moira to the water pipe. 'Why the water pipe?' says Tracey.

'A table then, or the counter – who cares, anywhere!'

Tracey thinks I'm joking. Moira is in the jolliest mood of her life. And when customers start arriving, they too wear eyeballs the size of pufferfish – no-one fails to notice that Moira is as desirable as oxygen.

I can't help but brush past her ten times a second. I can't help telling her that I'll die if the weekend passes without a whole lot of intimacy. Tracey tells me to cool it, offers me a large sausage to ram up my pussy, and says maybe we'll get friendly Sunday evening if nothing is interesting on television.

Two times before ten o'clock I had my phone in hand ready to call Joe. I'd brought his business card. I'm tired of the lost opportunities. Three whole days had passed and we could have been screwed silly and been walking like a jockey who'd lived for a year on a horse's back.

I told Moira that I may go to the riverbank in the afternoon. Another one of her giggles and she forbids me from going to the riverbank. Scarcely two minutes go by before a sexual innuendo spurts from my mouth but Tracey ignores me to purposely wind me up.

Hell, it's got to be the most unbearable shift ever. All those mornings in the past that I've ogled Lizzie's tits or felt frustrated with either Tracey or the previous incarnation of Moira, pale into nothingness compared with this. I recall having the hots for Lucy when I first saw her naked in the preparation room at SMA – even that yearning doesn't match this. Knowing it's Saturday exacerbates everything – there are almost 48 hours between now and Monday morning when the café opens again; believing those hours may be wasted is a crime against humanity. 'Let's close early and rush home to have an orgy… please.'

The girls show no compassion. Tracey cleans efficiently and does the things we always do on Saturday – checks the stock, scrubs the tiles, wipes the chair legs, scratches her ass, etc. And Moira continues to smile and flick her hair over her shoulder as if she's twisting the knot that's causing pain in my belly. 'Let's close early and screw Moira on top of the freezer… please.' Other than me, there's only Tracey who's ever touched Moira – she can't refuse such an offer.

The trade slows. The trade comes to an elongated end and when we're standing in a line behind the counter Tracey tells me I need an operation to remove my clitoris and Moira asks if that is one of my organs and am I poorly. We explain. Moira giggles. She's up to something but I have no idea what it is.

It can't get worse

Not only do I have to resist the luscious sight of Moira's bare legs on the front seat of the van while Tracey is driving home, but Lizzie greets us at the door in a dress that she bought last week from the clothes store, and she's wearing blue lipstick and smelling as sweet as sugary custard. 'The nymphomaniacs are back,' I say. Tracey's eyes light up as they swoop over Lizzie's body. I nudge Tracey and whisper in her ear, 'She's yours, I'm having Moira for lunch, dinner, and supper.'

I expect someone to make a move or announce that the waiting is over. We compliment Lizzie. Moira runs Lizzie's ponytail through her fingers and says the blue ribbon matches her lipstick; Lizzie looks beautiful. 'Have you something special planned?' she asks.

When Lizzie says 'No', Moira giggles again and then turns her attention to Tracey. 'And you?' she says. 'You're not going anywhere?'

Tracey's face betrays what she's thinking; her eyes dip to Lizzie's knees and she releases a tiny sigh. 'Nowhere in particular,' says Tracey.

It's as though we're stuck in a game but no-one's willing to reveal her hand. We're behaving like teenagers at a party and the host's mummy and daddy are squat on the landing.

Tracey goes to the kitchen to make a coffee; Lizzie and I sit on the sofa and Moira goes off to her bedroom. Fifteen minutes later, Tracey and I have changed out of our uniforms and we're back in the same positions but the initial warmth has settled into polite silence. In the corner of my eye, I can see the fabulous curves of Lizzie's tits and compare them to a sumptuous hot meal going steadily cold on a plate.

And that's it. Sitting in limbo with no hint of further progress. After suggesting we strip naked and run about the house to heat our blood, and getting not a word in response, I check the refrigerator for milk and the bread-bin for bread. I tell Tracey I'm going to the shop. 'Okay,' she says with zero interest. I collect my phone and jacket and wander out of the doorway like an unwanted guest. This restraint can't go on, and I'm determined to end it.

I go to the lane behind the church and sit on a tree stump that's been there since my childhood. No messing… I take from my pocket Joe's business card and hold the phone in my right hand. What do I say? 'Hi, Joe, gang-bangs on offer… buy one get one free. Anytime, anyplace, any number of participants… What do you say, Joe?'

He may not remember me. For all I know, he and his mates could hire a different girl every day or two. It's been a year or more… who knows. Perhaps he'll say I'm getting too old – 27 is stretching the imagination. Aren't you going through the menopause?

I convince myself that Joe WAS a nice guy. He liked me. His mates liked me. He told me to keep in touch. Do it, Rosa… press dial.

'Hi, Joe, it's me, Rosa.'

'No,' he says. 'Rosa from SMA?'

'Sure, little old me.'

'Rosa… I'm at the airport, just got back from New York… maybe you can call me in a day or two. Maybe we can do something… you know, that's if you're up for it.'

'Sure, Joe… a couple of days?'

'Yes, that would be perfect. Good to hear from you, girl. I look forward to your call.'

'I'll call you.'

'Okay, Rosa. Okay.'

Am I disappointed or leaving a stain on the tree stump? I'm not sure what to think. The background noise did indicate that Joe was in busy surroundings. Maybe he is interested. I can't believe I've called him. Is my body still fit enough to take a pounding from a dozen guys… six guys… twenty-five guys?

I go for the bread and milk and dawdle home half pleased, a quarter hesitant, and over a quarter scared. Sometimes when precious memories are revisited in reality the visitor gets an enormous shock. And by the time I'm placing the items in the kitchen, the over a quarter scared is now half scared+.

By late afternoon, we've all showered, had dinner, and interacted lovingly without a spark being ignited. I'm guessing the evening will pass as meaningfully as waiting at a bus stop for a canceled service.

Moira's invitation

Six-thirty and we're sitting in the room looking remotely like four girls who are deliberating whether to go out for a night on the town. No chance. They'll watch the television or spend hours listening to my pleas for sex before going to their bedrooms around 10. I make a joke about selling the dildos at a car boot sale, make another joke about us buying overalls, and they both fall flat. I think about calling on Uncle Russia but my excuses to go out are pathetic.

Six-forty, and I think my eyeballs are wobbling in their sockets. I rub them, then realize that Moira's legs are shaking and she's stretching her fingers as if she's got arthritis. I watch her but don't say anything.

Six-fifty, Moira's nervousness begins to show; she can't sit still and keeps sucking the end of her thumb. I'm about to ask her if she needs a massage or a cuddle under her duvet when she stands in front of the fireplace and says timidly, 'Would you all do me a very big favor, please?'

We're startled. 'BIG favor?' questions Tracey.

'I will,' says Lizzie.

I stare at Moira and she's wearing a foreign expression. I'm puzzled.

'I want you to go out, and you must not come back until 7.30. Exactly 7.30.' Moira's still shaking and begging us to do as requested.

'Is this a surprise?' asks Tracey.

'Please,' says Moira. 'Go for a walk, but don't return until 7.30. You must not come in until 7.30, no matter what.'

Tracey, Lizzie, and I look at each other like we're been sent out into a gale. We hesitate, question whether Moira is feeling well as she shoos us to the hallway as if she's afraid to make eye-contact.

Six-fifty-seven and we're walking in the direction of the church, coming up with theories as to what Moira is up to. It is some momentous day in her life? Can she shock us more than she shocked us with the hair dye?

We take Lizzie to the point on the lane where Tracey first assaulted me. We share memories of that significant moment, ask Lizzie if she'd like to lean against a tree and receive a double-handful. Lizzie looks gorgeous and Tracey is never far from her side. I'm sure they're screwing in secret but I'm not going to ask them if my suspicions are correct. I sense a little sexual chemistry in the air and start to hope that the evening will not pass uneventfully. When we get back, I'll encourage Tracey to take Lizzie to her bedroom.

We plod to the field, turn around, then dawdle back along the lane. Soon after we reach our street a car horn sounds and we see a hand wave from an open window. The car stops outside my house; it's only then that I think that it's Marty's car and the waving hand belongs to Katy. 'Oh no, not another apology,' says Tracey.

'If that's what they've come for, we're going out – whoring if necessary.' Tracey and Lizzie agree. We'd heard enough woe for a whole year.

As they get out of the car, we're quite surprised how smartly they're dressed. We pull faces at each other but don't speak until we're on the pavement outside my house. 'Waiting for 7.30?' asks Katy.

Marty looks at his watch. 'Two minutes yet,' he says.

I and the girls are flummoxed. 'Has Moira told you to come?' says Lizzie.

'What's the occasion?' asks Marty. 'Moira wouldn't tell us. We've left the girls at your parents.'

I'm speechless. Tracey throws out her open hands. 'Moira's had her first period,' jokes Lizzie. 'She's really thirteen and today is her birthday.'

No more guesses as to what's going on. We girls don't understand why Marty and Katy are here. We stand gawping at each other and wait for Moira to open the door at 7.30.

Moira's Sacrifice

'It's now 7.32,' says Marty with a touch of impatience.

I sidle to the door, press the handle, and put one foot inside the hallway before calling Moira in a loud whisper. No Moira.

'Shout her,' says Lizzie pushing at my back.

I'm thinking she's hiding with a party-popper primed for explosion. I step forward, say, 'I know you're there.'

The girls and Marty are huddled behind me and as we inch toward the room, we notice a giant banner fixed on the wall opposite the window. It's the creation Moira began earlier and it reads SIMPLE STORIES ARE THE BEST with a large arrow next to the word best that points to the hallway.

Marty says dumbly, 'We've just come from the hall.'

Then Tracey makes a silly noise as she glances up the stairway. 'There are arrows on the steps. Oh God, are you thinking what I'm thinking?'

'I dare not think,' I say. I feel instantly scared; Moira hasn't made a sound and for some mad reason, I dread that she's committed suicide. I push past Marty and Katy and squeeze Tracey's hand. She allows me to go first up the stairs. My legs are so heavy I can hardly lift them. None of us speak and by the time I reach the landing, my heart is pounding. A few more steps and we are gathering in my bedroom doorway and my dread turns to relief and astonishment. Somehow, Moira has got herself bound in the metal rods; they're attached to her ankles and wrists and her wrists are secured to the headboard. She's blindfolded, clad in those hideous white knickers and bra she wore when she first moved in. There are scissors on her belly and dildos and other sex toys strewn on the mattress. Lizzie giggles. Katy says, 'Oh, isn't she beautiful.'

I hurry to the top of the bed and pull the blindfold above Moira's eyes. 'What are you doing, girl?'

'Problems need fixing,' says Moira innocently. 'It's gone on too long. You're unhappy – we're all unhappy. Simple stories are the best – when folks have a problem, you find a resolution, and that's me. You can all screw me and then we can be happy again.'

'How sweet of you,' says Katy as Lizzie's curiosity is aroused by the various dildos and arms herself with a pair she's never seen before. Tracey is standing at the end of the bed assessing everyone's reaction. Marty hardly dares come through the doorway. My brain is telling me that Moira is a heroine and she's showing tremendous bravery for a girl who only ever had sex with me and Tracey, but my heart is turning green with jealousy and warning me that seeing my sweet little virgin being screwed by the five of us will just about kill me.

Lizzie giggles again and drops one of the dildos to replace it with the scissors. 'Can I have the pleasure?' she says snipping the scissor blades in the air. Tracey and Katy sit close to Moira's legs; they're smiling at her, probably unsure whether to proceed. Lizzie slices one side of the white knickers and exposes Moira's perfectly smooth mound.

'Put the blindfold over my eyes,' whispers Moira. My hands are shaking. As I lower the blindfold, I hear the scissors cut through Moira's knickers and in the corner of my eye see Tracey's fingers wander up Moira's leg. Pain lodges in my throat, I ask myself why Moira doesn't wish to see what's about to happen. Now both Katy and Tracey are fondling Moira and my left hand is trembling on her shoulder. 'It's okay, Mum,' she says, 'don't worry.'

But as soon as I hear Mum, I do not doubt that Moira is seeking help. If she truly wanted this, she'd say Rosa. She's doing this for us – it's her sacrifice, but I can't let it happen.

I pull the pole from under the headboard and start declaring that it should not be Moira who is doing this. I free Moira's wrists, remove the blindfold. There's a sigh from Lizzie but Katy and Tracey don't object. 'It should be me!' I yell. 'I'll make it up to all of you.'

Tracey laughs, 'You mean that you wish you'd thought of it.'

'No,' I snap. 'It shouldn't be Moira who's doing this.'

By now I've freed Moira's ankles and I'm lifting her to the side of the bed. When I raise my head, I see Lizzie's bra flying overhead; she's already removed her dress and a confident grin is etched on her face. She snatches the scissors, tilts her upper body backward and starts to cut off her knickers. 'Who started this, eh? I started it. I'm to blame. If anyone needs forgiveness, then it is me. You can all screw me – screw me as much as you like, and I'm not taking no for an answer.'

Lizzie dives on the bed, starts tossing the dildos at all of us, then spreads her legs and yells, 'And don't forget my tits.'

'How can we forget those tits,' says Marty boldly.

Tracey's eyes are beacons of delight. She's never minded sharing, and just as in the old days, she can't wait to spring to action. Moira glances as if to thank me. I cuddle her, and then for the first time a strange brain-fog envelops me – I've saved my sweet little virgin from being defiled and I'm having to pretend to be keen on satisfying Lizzie. In a state of numbness, I watch Tracey go down on Lizzie in a way she's not done for anyone in more than a year. Her reticence vanishes, she's hungry and adventurous. Surprisingly too, Katy joins the assault, willingly stretching Lizzie's legs and kissing the insides of her thighs as she works around Tracey's body. And even Marty moves to the end of the bed like he's hoping to gain access to Lizzie's pussy. I and Moira play peekaboo with the blindfold, occasionally kissing Lizzie, dipping our tongues in her mouth, or sucking her nipples. We work as a team but both without eagerness to swoop down her body; we hold hands, reassure each other that we're a separate couple who are doing this for the unity of the group.

And Lizzie loves this mass intrusion. She constantly lifts her head to peer through the blindfold that's risen to her forehead. She longs to see herself being licked and being impaled by the dildos that Tracey and Katy are using on her. Garments begin flying in all directions and Marty, less confidently than the girls, begins stripping. Moira and I prop Lizzie's head with pillows and tell her to enjoy the sight of her getting fucked. Moira climbs over her body so we can scream filthy words in each ear, and Lizzie's face is a picture of pleasure.

Katy and Tracey have bunged the duvet beneath Lizzie's ass so she's more accessible; they're driving into her and causing her to howl. The dildos push into her body and Moira and I sit on Lizzie's arms to add to her excitement.

I see Marty tap Katy on her ass, then he seeks permission to screw Lizzie. Tracey moves onto Lizzie's belly as Katy guides Marty toward Lizzie's wet hole. 'Give her more than you give me,' she says jokingly and she presses on his ass as he enters. Oh God, I never thought I'd see the day when Katy allowed him to screw anyone other than me.

And it turns into a frenzy of unrelenting sex as Marty, Katy, and Tracey share the entrances to Lizzie's desirable body. They alternate the dildos, they pummel her body with untold enjoyment and yell in success each time Lizzie produces more juice, and all the while I'm praying that they don't ask me or Moira to swap positions with them because Moira is mine and I'm so unwilling to share her. In many ways it's the most bizarre sex ever – I'm bewildered by my feelings. I'm more concerned about protecting Moira than finding sexual fulfillment.

But I must say that Lizzie used as the sacrifice for the prize of unity, came as the perfect choice. Her body is so appealing; she's the most irresistible of all of us. Sadly, no-one loves her although Tracey is warming to her, what she loses in lovability she makes up for with her figure, especially her tits and her adorably youthful pussy.

Lizzie takes all the filth from her pleasure providers and seems disappointed when Katy and Marty say that they must go to collect the children. We pause on the bed, jokingly tell our visitors that a second session will take place tomorrow. After many comments, the joke becomes a plan and we make a firm commitment to indulge in sex at the same time tomorrow evening. I agree with what they're saying but add the proviso that the action will be different – I'll think of something, but none of them is having my Moira.

And Katy and Marty leave and Tracey and I are left staring across the bed. Tracey's hand gently creeps to Lizzie's belly. 'You want more of her, don't you?' I say.

Lizzie lifts her head, 'Don't I get an opinion?'

'No,' Tracey says bossily. She picks up two dildos and crawls between Lizzie's legs.

I skirt the bed, pick up Moira in my arms. 'My sweet little girl's getting screwed in private,' I say. Moira smiles at Lizzie and Tracey, then off we go to Moira's bedroom. I'm going to give her so much love we won't rise from her bed until morning.

Early risers

What a night – moans rang out until the early hours; it became almost a competition as to which girl could be given the most orgasms. Tracey occasionally yelled from her bedroom that Lizzie had spurted to the farthest wall, and I'd yell that Moira's river had meandered down the stairs and flooded the kitchen. We screwed Lizzie and Moira in fabulous captivity and they even shouted to each other what was being done to their bodies. Sex after sex, sex to show the couple in the other bedroom that sex has no end. 'She's cum again,' Tracey would scream and I'd need to make Moira cum to get equal. Yes, we screwed them and used all our skills to make the night everlasting. It proved one of the best sex sessions ever, and each thrilling climax had me loving Moira a little bit more.

When I left Moira in her bed in the morning, she looked serene and her pale skin sported patches of dark pink on her thighs and all around her pussy. The upstairs smelled strongly of love-making. I went downstairs in the nude and found Tracey drinking coffee in the kitchen. She too hadn't bothered to dress. We gave each other a wicked look, then she leaned me over the table and shoved my knees wide apart. 'Five-minute lick,' she said, 'then you do it to me.'

But the five-minute lick got extended with a carrot taken from the refrigerator, and the five-minute lick that followed ended with me screwing Tracey on the sofa after I'd gone upstairs to find the strap-on. Tracey hadn't been so turned on for a century. Even when I'm screwing her, she goes on about Lizzie's body and apologizes for saying it's the best flesh she's ever fucked. I tell Tracey to go upstairs to continue her magical feast. But Tracey twists, kneels on the carpet and falls forward. She has me screwing her ass for the best part of thirty minutes while admitting she's not felt so horny since way back when, and she can't get enough of Lizzie. As I'm thrusting into her, she's asking me how she can go to London and leave Lizzie unattended, 'Oh God, she tastes exotic – I can't believe what she's done to me.'

And we make the downstair stink as pungently as the upstairs, and for a few more minutes I get Tracey to put on the strap-on and screw me on the table. We deliberate about going to the bedrooms and giving the girls a reason to wake up happy. We screw some more before eventually making a coffee and sitting side by side on the sofa with our hands still wandering. This is sure like the time after we first got together and Tracey grudgingly regrets that she allowed business affairs to take over her life.

Then Tracey begins a soliloquy about Lizzie's glorious light pink pussy, her hips, her belly, her neck, her shoulders, and her amazing tits. She turns herself on by her imaginings and I'm having to poke her to keep the words spilling from her mouth. She tells me how much she loves me but love has nothing to do with sexual attraction. I ask if she has feelings for Lizzie; she isn't sure – she wants more of her, lots more of her and she confesses that Lizzie has changed and her nature is sweeter and kinder because of my counseling.

Tracey asks about Moira, and I admit that I'm madly in love with her – I'm jealously possessive and I can't bear the thought of someone touching her. Tracey guessed that from my behavior and she doesn't mind. Then she shuffles her body and rearranges my limbs so that I'm half laid on the sofa facing the ceiling. She starts to poke me and demands that I must tell her the joys of Moira's body while she brings me to orgasm. If I don't produce an orgasm she'll run upstairs and inform Moira that I begged to be screwed with the carrot and the strap-on before Moira gets from her bed.

A fantastic early morning follows a fantastic night. We're back on track. My hopes for endless days of stunning sex are high, and Tracey has to wash her sticky face in the kitchen sink.

What we've missed out on

For most of the day, we float about wearing only a bra and our knickers. We're like love-sick doves, flapping and pecking, not needing reasons to touch each other's skin. Tracey follows Lizzie, I follow Moira. Lizzie follows Tracey and Moira follows me. Every few minutes there are passionate kisses. We lean each other on walls. One sits on the table trapping the other's body in her thighs. We share showers. We get naked for a while then again put on our underwear.

There are countless declarations of love and an infinite number of wanton requests for sex. Once in a while one of us asks what we're going to do tonight – there's a suggestion that we all screw Katy, and Lizzie comes up with the idea of tying Marty to the bed to see how many of us he can handle before going floppy.

We're proud of each other when noon comes and we find time to eat a sandwich and have another coffee while sitting on separate chairs. But after fifteen minutes, those old feelings of neglect get us tossing the plates and cups in the kitchen sink and going through to the room. As Tracey and I follow the girls behind the sofa, we suddenly dive forward and pull down their knickers; they giggle and attempt to run toward the stairway. We grab their bra straps and haul them to the front of the sofa, yank off their bras and force them to recline with their legs locked in our arms. God, Tracey, and I just stare at their bodies; I can't say what Tracey's thinking but I see the most gorgeous creature in the universe whose newly blonde hair is straggled over her shoulders and the curly bits on the end are curving over her tiny tits. I could spend my life gazing at her; she's faultless and my belly is inflated with love. Moira wraps my hair around her fingers and says playfully, 'What are you two wicked witches going to do to us?'

'You haven't touched us for months,' says Lizzie teasingly as she attempts to spread her legs on the edge of the cushions.

Tracey's vibrating, she has her thumbs cupped on Lizzie's thighs and is severely drunk with lust. 'Eat her,' I say.

Moira and Lizzie let out an exaggerated moan and jerk their asses to indicate where they want us to go. 'You can't resist,' says Lizzie with a laugh.

And Tracey doesn't resist. Moira and I watch as she sinks her lips on Lizzie's pussy and begins sucking hungrily on the top part of her slit. It's instantly jaw-dropping, such a splendid display of unconstrained lust that I and Moira forget everything and concentrate on the spectacle and adore each noisy slurp and the open body of Lizzie rippling with excitement. As we watch, an idea for tonight jumps into my thoughts. I think about my father watching the film of my gang-bang at the Golf Club. I never knew until now how much pleasure is derived from seeing others have sex. And when I glance at Lizzie's bulging lips, I realize that moistness is gathering in my body and I'm almost as turned on as she is.

Moira tugs on my hair, 'Please...' she whispers. I want to keep watching but the desire to taste Moira overwhelms me. When Lizzie emits a deep satisfied groan, I leap to my feet, seize Moira's hands, and drag her upstairs to her bedroom. I throw myself on her bed, and as she climbs on me, I heave her thighs to my face and steer her to seek comfort in mine. Oh, this moment of extreme lust shall live forever as a treasured memory. That first taste of her is sublime. And when I sense her tongue inside me, I know I'm alive in Heaven.

Up for an Oscar

We're larking about, bragging that our athletic prowess should take us to the next Olympics and win us gold medals in sexual endurance events, when Katy and Marty arrive just after 7.30. Katy has made a special effort to look glamorous; she's wearing a short skirt that covers one-fifth of her extra-long legs. Her revealing blouse is daring and I can tell that she's up for almost anything. For once, Marty appears relaxed and immediately asks what's on the agenda. Lizzie goads him, says he's screwing five girls' asses – and that's just the appetizer.

We're all jolly, sitting then standing to talk, popping in the kitchen for a glass of gin or a can of lager and a nibble from a small selection of food. They seem to be expecting me to announce a timetable as if it's a play at the theater. Tracey jokes that we'll get in the back of the MAID MOIRA'S van – Moira's going to drive and the rest of us can have mobile sex which should be fun when we go over speedbumps.

After twenty minutes Katy reminds me that her girls are at our parents' and they've not got all evening for small-talk. When she gives me one of those big-sisterly looks, I get kind of nervous about declaring what I've got in mind. She says that she can't believe that she's come for a second helping and tells me how disgusted our parents would be if they knew what was going on here. I tap her arm, and suddenly notice Tracey fondling Lizzie's ass – maybe that's the signal for activities to commence?

'Okay,' I say loudly and pat my hands so everyone settles in a seat. Seconds later, five sets of eyes are staring at me and I'm not confident that my idea is going to be without objections. 'First, there's the location...' I point to the rug in front of the fireplace, 'there, or the bedroom?'

There's a stony silence before Tracey says there isn't much space on the rug. I suggest pushing the sofa toward the back wall and putting the rug in the center of the room. There are lots of whispers; the rug gains a majority 4-2 decision but no-one seems delighted at the thought of a pile-up of bodies on a six by four spread of wool.

I sit forward, display two rows of teeth, then hold out my phone on the end of a shaking arm. 'Show me your phones,' I say as my heart pounds.

One by one, phones appear in front of startled faces. Only Tracey seems comfortable with where I'm going. 'Your imagination...' she says cheekily.

I go in for the kill. 'We're going to create a keepsake. Now that we're happy again, I can see Katy and Marty returning to matrimonial bliss. Tracey will be embroiled in her business affairs, and even though Lizzie hasn't said that she's staying forever, I hope she does. Last night and this evening will just be memories. But memories don't have to vanish with these things,' I say while wobbling the phone in my hand.

'Hell's bells!' cries Lizzie. 'We're making a porn movie!'

'A beautiful keepsake,' I say.

Horror whitens Katy's cheeks and Marty looks anxious.

While I assess the reaction, I tell them my plan: pull back the sofa, center the rug, Tracey and Lizzie start screwing with the remaining four filming them. Don't waste filming time – storage isn't endless, capture good bits. Then we film Katy and Marty, and then me and Moira. Filthy, wonderful sex scenes that Moira can put together on her computer and make into a film. 'Well...' I say, 'who's up for it?'

A resolute 'yes' from Lizzie. Tracey laughs and gives her approval. Moira smiles sweetly and says that she'll do it. Marty looks open-eyed at Katy. Katy says grudgingly, 'I'll do it providing that my face is not shown on the final film.' Then Marty raises his thumb. I don't waste another second and do not hesitate in pushing the sofa to the far wall and lifting the rug to the center of the room. 'Let's get screwing,' I yell, 'Tracey, Lizzie… the rug is all yours.'

Oh God, for the first few minutes I'm not quite sure how it's going to play out. Katy's expression reeks of uncertainty and Marty is fumbling with his phone as if he's going to come up with an excuse why he can't film. As Tracey gets to grips with Lizzie – both still standing – me and Moira crouch on the carpet with our phones at the ready, waiting to capture some noteworthy action. But as soon as Lizzie's top comes off and Tracey plays out a sexy scene of removing Lizzie's knickers with her teeth, things step up a beat. Lizzie's body's an instant turn-on and seeing Tracey suck hard on Lizzie's nipples is the first wonderful capture.

Tracey's skills shine brightly; she knows instinctively that she's performing for a lens and her acting, as opposed to the quenching of her desires, is her priority. She maneuvers Lizzie's limbs for the benefit of the cameras, highlights her moans with heavy breathing and encourages Lizzie to do the same. Soon Katy and Marty are selecting choice angles, and with Moira and me, we work as a team to record the erotic moments.

From what could have been a disaster, superb lust rises as our porn stars perform magnificent sexual acts. I slap ass-cheeks to leave imprints of a hand, I shout filthy phrases and go in for close-ups when gaps appear between their bodies. However, I'm constantly aware that the capacity of phones is limited.

I don't wish to give the impression that this experiment went perfectly – it didn't. I'll reserve judgment on Katy and Marty's efforts, and I've got to say that after I and Moira performed promisingly for four or five minutes, we turned the porn movie into some kind of farce. The mischievous foursome of Tracey, Lizzie, Katy, and Marty tried repeatedly to grope Moira's body – sure, probably for fun, but jealous Rosa reacted defensively and protected her little girl by sprawling over her, fending off poking fingers, swiping at invading limbs and generally trying to be a shell over a naked sweet tortoise. When they failed to get to Moira, they got to me, and the sensational film that was supposed to be our objective became a hilarious comedy that ended with me covering Moira with cushions from the sofa so the evil foursome couldn't get to her.

Yes, we laughed stupidly and danced around the room in a happy celebration. I can't say we didn't have a good time. No-one moaned and it enforced our thinking that the many weeks of awkwardness had ended, but it didn't exactly induce calls for a re-run and nor did it advertise the benefits of group sex.

Afterthoughts

As on Saturday evening, after Katy and Marty left, Tracey led Lizzie upstairs to continue their physical adventure; Tracey looked as horny as hell and said Lizzie won't be attending the café in the morning because she'll still be screwing her. I and Moira went to her small bedroom and laid on top of the duvet to cuddle like a pair of love-struck bunnies. She thanked me for defending her and called me 'Rosa the Protector' as if I were some heroic historical figure. We had what may be described as gentle sex, in the darkness, to the background sound of moans coming from the next bedroom on the landing. Although Moira was no more than a silhouette on a gray background, I just kept thinking how beautiful she is, how she looks so grown up since dying her hair, and how of all my lovers, she's the gentlest and the easiest to feel at ease with. I think we're fated to be together forever.

And that's what occupied my mind until long after Moira fell asleep in my arms with her face molded into my breasts. I recalled the recent past, from the time I was paying Harry to have sex with me on the tower block roof to my visits to Uncle Russia's apartment. There were secret short sessions with Lizzie and Tracey, perhaps a nibble of Katy, and lost opportunities to have sex with Marty. Then those barren weeks, aching to be satisfied and having only myself to rely on. Sure, Moira comforted me, but not enough to prevent me from planning a reunion with Joe and his mates. I yearned for sex more than I ever yearned for food.

Those barren weeks ended with Moira's Saturday evening sacrifice when her 'Simple Story' persuaded her to lay in my bed wearing those unflattering knickers and bra. Yes, it turned out that we screwed Lizzie instead, but it's down to Moira that we're all speaking and once more enjoying what all humans are put on this earth to do. Two other things Moira has done add stardust to her sacrifice – I hadn't reckoned on the effect on me of the hair dye, and neither did I expect that the dropping of the 'Mum' title (it's almost stopped completely) would somehow strengthen my love for her. If I'm honest, I'm madly in love. I want to be near her every hour of every day.

I expected that when the abstinence ended, we four girls would indulge in daily orgies, and on the side, I'd be going for extra helpings with perhaps, Katy, Marty, Uncle Russia, and possibly Sally. I thought that sex would flow from all quarters – I could love Tracey and Moira and be satisfied by a host of willing lovers. I am wrong. These past two evenings threaten lasting changes that may determine the course of all our lives.

Let me explain… As individuals, I believe that distinctive lessons have been drawn from the past evenings' experiences. Katy longed to establish the true relationship between Marty and me. She assumed we were physically close and wanted to see Marty's reactions when set free to indulge in group sex. As for Marty, perhaps he'd have wished to see me show interest in him. He was disappointed and learned that my love for Moira is far deeper than it ever was for him. They turned to each other. And so… I expect my sister and my former partner will distance themselves from me and the girls – they'll return to being a couple and console themselves with the thought their relationship is secure.

As for Tracey… Tracey doesn't compete for love; she's happy with our open relationship and quite content finding sexual freedom with Lizzie. Half her mind is trapped in business affairs – as far as I know, she's no wish to fall in love with anyone else because she may be temporarily leaving us when she goes off to London; only time will tell.

And that leaves Lizzie. Lizzie has three choices. She's never committed to staying here forever, but if she wants to, that's fine. When Tracey goes, if that's what happens, she could return to Uncle Russia's or possibly head south with Tracey.

I suppose what I'm saying is that six folks have turned into three pairings, and tonight, I envisage that's how it's going to stay. A new future beckons – if I had to bet, I'd say that pretty soon I and Moira shall be sleeping between two empty bedrooms.

Words with Moira

Monday morning is always busy; regular customers flood through the door as if they haven't eaten since Saturday, and with only two of us on shift we scarcely had time to scratch our heads until well after 10.30. Moira, who slept like a log, kept complaining that Tracey and Lizzie made too much noise and she barely closed her eyes.

She looked extra-gorgeous in her uniform; her new blonde hair contrasted beautifully on the red material and a couple of times I bumped into the sharp edge of the counter because I wasn't looking where I stepped, instead, transfixed on Moira's eyes and mouth and wishing we were still cuddled up in bed whispering sweet nothings.

When we eventually made a coffee and leaned over the counter staring at the empty tables and chairs, Moira said suddenly, 'I would have done it, you know.'

I had no idea what she was talking about. I assumed she maybe meant she'd have cooked the last bacon sandwich. I thought for a few seconds then joked, 'You're lazy.'

She looked puzzled, then repeated her statement but this time emphasizing 'done it'. She added, 'I thought about it all week. Someone had to do something. There was an officer at the children's home who used to say that simple stories are the best, and I got thinking about what he meant by that. He also used to say that all problems have solutions. I put two and two together and came up with my plan.'

'Oh, Saturday evening,' I said stupidly.

'Yes, what do you think I was referring to? Saturday evening when you all found me on your bed... did you like the old knickers and bra idea?'

'You're so thoughtful. You did it for me. You'd have let Katy, Marty, Lizzie, and Tracey share your body, just for me.'

'We couldn't go on like that. You looked so miserable. I love you, Rosa, I'd do anything for you.'

'I know, sweetheart. I love you too. I'm so glad it didn't happen.'

'I'd have let them do what they wanted to me. I wouldn't have complained so long as it ended up as us all being friends. The sex was a price worth paying to see you smile again and so you could visit me in my bed again without the others objecting.'

'But you didn't want sex, did you? Not for yourself?'

'Why?' said Moira ever so quietly.

'You called me Mum. 'It's okay Mum, don't worry' you said. You didn't say Rosa, you were asking for help.'

Moira smiled, looked at me with an amazed expression, 'Can you read minds?'

'Your mind… maybe.'

'It wasn't the sex that bothered me,' said Moira, 'but having sex with folks I know – folks that know both of us – Lizzie, Katy, and Marty! They'd think that in the future they'd have some claim on me. They'd think that they could have me again, and maybe again. I don't belong to them; I belong to you… and a tiny bit to Tracey. I chickened out, didn't I?'

The café was empty. I took Moira into the back area and leaned her against the freezer and gave her the most passionate lasting kiss I've ever given anyone. Oh God, love was bursting my belly and my heart throbbed with her heart and I wanted to hold her forever. 'I'll never expect you to share your body with anyone,' I said.

'I know now I'd never share it with those around us,' she giggled.

My eyes lit up and I thought I was making a joke when I said, 'You'd share it with strangers?'

'Have gang-bangs as you've had?' said Moira still giggling.

We started making light of the moment. 'Hey, get a job in the cages at SMA.'

'Yes, I'll be a specialist in gang-bangs,' said Moira.

'On tables.'

'On anything…'

'No one-inch dicks,'

'Donkey-length only.'

We kissed some more and played with each other's clothes like we pretended to be a pair of whores getting ready for a party. We got interrupted by a late customer who wanted a sausage sandwich. 'Don't we all?' I said to him which got Moira giggling hysterically. And after he left, we became normal again, but I wondered if things went on in Moira's head that I didn't know about. It sounded as though she'd thought about sex more than I've given her credit for.

More food for thought

Moira drove us home at a steady pace with me gawping at her legs throughout the journey. I thought how lucky I am, thought back to that moment outside the SMA building when I first put my hand under her dress. I didn't know then that she'd bloom and become so fabulous and that I'd find myself almost glued to her side. Even exiting the van by opposite doors seemed an act of separation. I soon skipped to join her and we entered the house together and yelled up the stairs, 'Wake up, we're back!'

But there were noises in the kitchen, and we crossed the room and pushed open the door. Kneeling naked on a chair with a beastly contraption around her hips was Lizzie pumping into Tracey fully-clothed apart from knickers sprawled on the kitchen table. Lizzie didn't pause but kept her eyes on Tracey's pussy as she nodded a welcome.

'Bacon, egg & tomato, please,' joked Moira.

We stood as spectators, listened to Tracey's moans, and watched her arms flail in excitement and the sweat roll off her brow and drip onto the table's surface. I've got to say, that watching Lizzie's tits while she rocks her body is a spectacle; they're so firm and solid they're like crafted masterpieces made by an angel. She folded back her shoulders as an offer for us to suck them, but just as she does, Tracey's phone on the work surface rings.

I pass the phone to Tracey. It's hilarious… a moan, then 'yes', moan, 'Oh, Angela', moan 'Oh, God, moan, 'I'm being screwed,' moan, moan, 'I'll call you back when I'm done.' If anything, it looks more like Lizzie's heading for a climax, her lips are full and her tongue is licking the air. She drives harder into Tracey and Tracey is pushing a single finger up in the air to say, 'just another minute.' Moira darts to the cupboard and returns with the tomato ketchup and squirts it all over Tracey's pussy.

'Your period's started…' we shout merrily. And we spoil the moment; the screwing stops but there are no ill-feelings. Both Tracey and Lizzie claim they've now got sufficient reason to carry on screwing in the shower, then after that in bed.

As they go upstairs, I help Moira wipe the table and simultaneously our eyes fall on Tracey's phone. 'Angela., she's not leaving Tracey alone,' I say. 'I think she'll be going to London.'

'I'll never leave you,' says Moira. She curls her little finger around mine. 'Lovers forever.'

'Let's go to bed,' I say.

'Why not,' says Moira.

Unspoken arrangements

Lots of things in life just happen. Folks instinctively interact without verbal explanations. We take for granted that loved ones are preparing their future days without specifically questioning their motives or why there have been no long-drawn-out conversations on what they intend to do.

I got my bed back. Tracey took refuge on Lizzie's three-quarter mattress without leaving a forwarding address. She upped and went on Tuesday afternoon to sink between Lizzie's thighs like they were friendly blankets that shielded her from cross-examination. That doesn't mean she neglected me – oh no, from 3 p.m. to 5 p.m. that very day, I and Tracey screwed Lizzie's ass alternately; we bound her in Marty's pink straps and gorged on her delicious body while Moira played on her laptop downstairs. We treated Lizzie like she was a piece of succulent meat, feasting on both ends of her, making her ass go scarlet as we strove to give her innumerable orgasms. And we were successful, and Lizzie was delirious and appreciative and stayed open-legged in bed long after I came downstairs. Tracey promised her more sex, promised to screw her all evening if I'd make them sandwiches and take them to their bedroom.

And like a good servant, I made the sandwiches, delivered them, then came to stand in front of the fireplace to gaze longingly at Moira who was now sitting quietly on the sofa. Some kind of bossy mood enveloped me. I found myself uttering dirty remarks. One after another I came out with disgusting ideas of what I may do to Moira's body: impale her on a cucumber, make her strip naked and stand at the open front door – I'd poke her from behind while folks pass the house. I suggested displaying her stood on chairs at the window while I used the big black dildo to excite her. I said I'd force her to masturbate until she squirted all over my face.

Moira simply stared at me with dull eyes. Rightly or wrongly, I thought I was turning her on. So, I continued and came out with the vilest things I could do to her – worse than I've mentioned. I kept asking if she wanted me to be abusive, be rough with her, and screw her so badly that her pussy would throb for days. Sure, Moira's juices were flowing, and so were mine. Without asking, she began shuffling out of her clothes, tossing each item at my face, and saying things she'd like me to do to her. Her voice became sharper and she uttered my name twenty times; she knows that calling me Rosa, instead of Mum, gets me going. 'Strip for me, Rosa.' 'Let me see you, Rosa.' 'You want this, Rosa,' she said extending her tongue. And when I stood naked leering at her exposed body, she placed her hands on her thighs and separated her hidden flesh.

Indecency consumed my brain and I snatched her hand and took her to the rear garden. There, we had wild sex on the bench, on the lawn, and even leaning against the wall of the house. Sure, from some angles, if neighbors were at their upstairs windows, they could see us, but I didn't care. The desire to screw Moira proved irresistible; I had to see her panting, see that gorgeous face expressing ultimate pleasure. And she did to me what I did to her and we screwed until our bodies were exhausted. Life seemed to have become what I've craved for, and we swore to have sex again before nightfall.

These few days after the crazy weekend were manic. On Wednesday I and Moira had sex on a table in the café after closing time. We stopped at the local shop on the way home and saw Uncle Russia swinging a loaf of bread like it was one of those toys that makes a high-pitched noise as it whirls. He asked over Lizzie. I told him Lizzie was okay and I'd tell her I'd seen him. He glanced at my thighs as if to suggest that sex is available if I want it. I nodded, but right now, I'm not tempted to accept.

Then we got home. The phone rings, and it's Katy. Katy talks about her girls, what they're doing at school, she mentions some cut-price coats at the clothes store near the precinct, and how she's just received a pay-rise. No word of Marty, no talk of sex, and she ends the call with a 'Take care, sis.' I knew she'd keep her distance – at least she and Marty are probably screwing again.

And Moira and I screwed again, on the sofa, with Tracey and Lizzie going to and fro from the upstairs to the kitchen. It was as if we were seeing which pair could have the most sex. It was as if we'd taken it for granted that every spare minute, we'd rip off each other's clothes (when we wore clothes) and make the house stink a little more. No time for cleaning, but time to discover whether another orgasm is possible.

We got close to a foursome when passing each other in the hall. Lizzie was on top of Tracey on the lower steps and for a few minutes, Moira and I joined the action. The oddest thing about this brief encounter was that none of us spoke; rapid pokes, heavy squeezes, and lashing tongues, then Moira and I resumed sex in the shower.

It became obvious by Thursday that Tracey is bound for London. She'd taken phone calls in private, talked like she'd told us every detail of what lay ahead. Even a suitcase had been packed and stored on the landing. I didn't confront her, I refused to ask, 'Are you leaving me?'

Oh, several times, we exchanged those glances that emit love and a hint of unspoken guilt. She didn't wish to hear her voice telling me she is going. I didn't wish to hear it either. Just go. Say you'll be back in a month or two. Say you can live on love in your heart, we can have sex in the future. Tracey, I promise you I'll keep on

screwing Moira, maybe sometimes I'll believe she is you. Our love
will never die. Tell me that you're taking Lizzie to keep your body
occupied when days are lonely and you're thinking of me.

It got to Friday and no-one questioned the reason
why we all went to the café. Even the customers noticed the staff
overcrowding. At one point there was so little room behind the
counter that I took Tracey into the back of the premises and
molested her lower half as she laid on the freezer. She kept saying
'I'm going to miss you' like it was an order for me to use my fingers a
little more forcefully like she wanted to leave her scent on the
enamel coating so I'd smell her even when I'm working. A short
while later I'm kissing Lizzie while pressing her body against the
water pipe and I remind her about the barbed wire, shaving her
pussy, and her biting my ass.

Everything is insane: why don't we communicate? Why don't
I ask when Tracey is going and if she is taking Lizzie with her?

The insanity persisted; the most bizarre afternoon of my
entire life follows...

Going-away present

Around three o'clock Tracey comes from the kitchen carrying a tray
loaded with snacks, two bottles of gin, and four glasses. She hasn't
forewarned us of a special occasion; we're fully dressed, perhaps
enjoying a respite from sex and I feel sure that Moira is thinking
about her computer – she's been trying to make something of the
film snips from last Sunday evening but she's previously said they are
a great disappointment.

'Is your bed available?' asks Tracey.

'Who wants it?' I say.

Tracey shakes the tray, invites us to inspect its content, then beckons us with a flick of the head – we must follow; it's perhaps our final chance to say what we've stored in our heads or rid our bodies of any unquenched desires. No questions, complete obeyance like she's head of the sect and we dare not argue. We follow her upstairs in single file, no touching asses on the steps and no accompanying whispers or sighs. We sit on the bed; from left to right, Lizzie, Tracey, me, then Moira, and almost immediately Tracey's pouring gin and handing each of us a full glass. Then we're instructed to grab a handful of nibbles and to 'be happy'.

Slurps, chomping, crisps crushed by teeth, shifting limbs, furtive glances like we're wondering what each other's thinking, and lots of hair-flicking like we're all urging Tracey to make an announcement. I expect her to tell us that she's going to London in the morning. She'll be away for x-number of months, we had better miss her, her place in one or another bed will never be taken by an intruder. She may burst into tears and claim her trip is necessary to secure our financial future.

And the last point hits the bullseye. Tracey takes a mouthful of gin, then says, 'Girls, we're going to be rich – richer than you can ever imagine.'

'I think we're rich already,' says Moira.

'Me too,' says Lizzie. 'We get our wages from the café and we never get a chance to spend them. I've never been so loaded.'

'Things will get even better,' says Tracey. 'You'll see...'

I glimpse the edge of Tracey's suitcase on the landing and she notices me looking. 'Packed...' I say sorrowfully. She kisses the side of my head. 'Remember girl, I love you more than I've ever loved anyone. Someday, maybe in the autumn, I'll take you back to the lane behind the church and remind you of how it all started.'

For the first time, I get the impression that Tracey has something up her sleeve. She empties her glass, pours a refill, and tops up our glasses with gin. Then she starts waffling about her past, going from her early years screwing in the schoolyard to her nights in town and her adventures with locals. She refers to our gang-bang at the Golf Club, to the cages at SMA, and rabbits on for ages about how I and Moira brought her back to fitness after her accident. She never thought she'd walk normally again after breaking her femur when falling from the harness in one of the SMA rooms. 'You two nursed me back to life,' she says before taking another large gulp of gin.

Tracey usually drinks lager, and the strength of the gin soon has her slurring words. The rest of us are like three kids been entertained by a favorite aunt. We smile, say little, and allow Tracey to continue with her ramblings.

She laughs suddenly, looks at each of us in turn, then says, 'Hey, isn't it wonderful eh – my three most treasured pussies all in the same bed.' She goes on to describe what we taste like, how our pussies differ, how I came first, then Moira, then Lizzie. She boasts that she knows the exact location of our sweet spots, where to touch us to get the best reaction, and how she knows when each one of us is close to orgasm and what she will do next to ensure that we squirt. She admits that she'd have had more sex with Moira had it not been for my possessiveness. She says that this past week bathing in Lizzie's juices have provided some highlights of her life – 'My screwing days were over,' she declared, 'but God, when I saw Lizzie's tits and her cute girlie slit, I sprang back to life like a jack-in-a-box. When I die and get cremated, I'll have my ashes buried between Lizzie's legs.'

She goes on rambling, pours yet more gin into her glass, and records details of our sex acts like they've happened minutes ago. She explains what we do with our faces, how our bellies suck breath differently, how we stiffen our legs and betray sensations through our fingers, she picks out her favorite parts of our bodies and says my ass is the one ass she'd choose from all the asses in the world. And then I get a clue of where this is leading... She explains the nuances of sex when she watches me and Moira or me and Lizzie, she says how her sex has this or that aspect with each one of us – whichever couple is screwing she can foresee what's going to happen and she gets a kick out of being correct. 'I love watching you guys,' she says, 'but if I've got one regret, it is this...'

Oh God, I'm certain of what she's about to say. I'm ambivalent. Say it. Don't say it. Please request it. Don't dare open your mouth.

Drunkenly, Tracey puts her face close to mine and licks the end of my nose. She wears a stupid grin and tells me that I've longed to see the same as she's longed to see but I'm too damned obsessive to let it happen. 'You'd love to see it but you're chicken, Rosa.' Then she flings up her arms spilling the tiny amount of gin in her glass, and declares, 'Admit it, girl.'

'What has she to admit?' asks Moira.

'Don't ask me,' says Lizzie.

Tracey belches. She nips my chin in her fingers. 'If there's anything in the world that would give you and me an almighty orgasm, what would it be? Be fucking honest. Say it, or I'll say it for you.'

'I'm saying shit.' Yes, I'm certain what's coming. There are knots in my belly and I'm staring into Tracey's eyes with fear and with sublime anticipation.

Tracey struggles to the bottom of the bed, puts the tray on the floor and takes the glasses from everyone's hands. Then she leans forward, hoists me toward her until I fall onto the carpet before standing at her side. Tracey points at Lizzie, then she points at Moira.

'Rosa Saint John, if there's one thing that would do to us more than it would do for them, is...'

Lizzie and Moira exchange glances. Now they know what's coming too.

'You strip your girl, and I'll strip mine,' says Tracey.

Lizzie's eyes sparkle. Moira looks from the top of her eyes at me. 'If you'd both like to watch me and Lizzie having sex... yes, I'll do it,' says Moira.

Tracey holds her pussy and yells, 'Oh God, it's a dream come true. Rosa, you're about to explode.'

We hesitate before going to separate sides of the bed and kind of nervously begin taking off Lizzie and Moira's skirts and tops. When they're in their underwear, we kneel them to face each other and give them time to anticipate the first moves. Tracey is as horny as me when we take off their bras and then their knickers. We come to the end of the bed and hold each other; our bodies shake uncontrollably as the girls move forward and start caressing each other's tits.

My throat burns, sensations swarm in my body as the girls' caresses become more intimate. Tracey is moaning like she's being screwed in every orifice and she's already tearing at our clothes. And when Lizzie lays Moira on her back and meanders all over her body Tracey throws off her top and tries to say what she wants me to do to her while watching. We don't know what to do; the scene is so mind-blowing our limbs can barely function. Imagine the sexiest body you've ever seen screwing the person you love the most. Jesus! We strip off but even in our nakedness the pleasure is not enough and we're doubly drunk with excitement as Lizzie goes down on Moira and Moira makes noises like she's entering paradise. I'm not ashamed to say that me and Tracey search for ideal viewing spots. We try to poke each other but find that poking ourselves is more arousing. The girls move; neither pays heed to us, they consume each other, let their fingers and tongues run amok on their silky flesh, let their faces be wettened and smothered, let their limbs flex and relax and wrap and intertwine while I and Tracey use our skills to bring moisture to our pussies. And when Moira gets astride Lizzie and slides up her body leaving trails of pleasure in a snaking line, we run to each other and squat on the bed close to Lizzie's head. We're in a small circle, moaning, leaking, glorying in the sight of each's lover being satisfied in the astonishing depravity that is sex. Moira gyrates on Lizzie's mouth and my resistance to abstain diminishes. In her inebriated state, Tracey falls forward; I go to catch her and six arms meet in a net of comfort. We tangle, awkwardly grope in the thick of desire before two distinct pairings become one mass of four that swims in the realms of pleasure as the clock ticks continuously toward tomorrow.

Sex went on and on, and as it progressed, I stopped reaping the thrill of Moira sacrificing her body to Lizzie but dwelt on the ramifications of Tracey's goodbye. She must be pained, she must hurt inside as she's never hurt before – the drunkenness, the concealment of the truth that she's leaving and this is our final act of togetherness. She prefers to hide beneath a canopy of tingling skin rather than admit that the lure of ambition is stronger than the will to be physically embroiled. Sure, I know she's doing it for all of us – this obsession to live in financial comfort never leaves her for long.

I wish she'd whisper, 'I'll return in a month or return in two months.' I wish she'd tell all of us that this forthcoming change will only be temporary – the sun will bounce from the horizon and very soon everything will return to normal.

But Tracey, more than any of us, keeps the sex going – she dares not stop even if sobriety takes her. She fears explanation and fends off questions with a shield of impenetrable lust. She will still love me tomorrow and the days that follow but losing her shall be difficult.

She was my woman... I let her go...

Pass me your confidence to dress in my uniform, my sweet little maid. Pass me your smile as we cross the landing where Tracey's suitcase sits. Pass me your hopes over breakfast. Pass me your courage to lock the door. Pass me solace, pass me compassion as we drive to the precinct. Pass me your hand. Pass me the keys and pass me the strength to open the shutters.

Morning at MAID MOIRA'S, never more hushed, never more sorrowful, never more lethargic. We serve customers, let our tears fall out of sight next to the freezer. We show our teeth to please, exhibit fake smiles on frozen faces, deliver orders. as if we are robots and the unheard thud of our hearts interrupts hundreds of fractured movements. 'I love you, Moira.'

'I love you, Rosa.'

'We're down to the last pack of sausages.'

'There are tears in my shoes.'

'I dread the silence.'

'Life goes on.'

'Not as we know it.'

'I have you, Rosa.'

'I have you, my darling girl.'

And morning floats by – a log on a still pond, a car trapped in snow, minute by minute aching for truth when the truth is already apparent. The last customer leaves, dawdling to delay the turn of the closed sign. He looks back to ascertain if he's left any possessions on the table. 'You've got everything,' says Moira.

Last cleans. Last wipes. Last mopping of the floor. 'Ready,' I say.

We trudge to the van. The door is heavy. 'The sausages can wait,' says Moira.

20 m.p.h. slower than usual. Passing the church, I scan the back lane for signs of Tracey. I take the door key from my pocket and feel its shape with my fingers. Moira pulls to a halt. We touch hands before alighting.

The front door hasn't changed; the light is on in the hall. Key in lock. Twist. Open. Welcome to nothingness. Welcome to silence. I run upstairs, call to Moira, 'It's gone.'

'The suitcase?' she says with her face pointing up the stairs.

We enter the room. On the sofa are two large bouquets, two heart-shaped boxes of chocolates, and two envelopes. We open the envelopes; inside each is two thousand pounds in cash and a note reading, 'Overtime paid in advance XXX.'

Moira notices a message attached to the bouquets, 'Love Tracy and Lizzie.'

'They've both gone,' I murmur.

I take Moira's hand and lead her upstairs to our bedroom. We fall on the bed, embrace like children deserted by their parents, then cry our eyes out until they are sore.

Another use for the kitchen table

We're not used to sitting on straight-back chairs and staring across the kitchen table like civilized folks who don't eat their dinner from their laps. Moira jabs her fork into a piece of tomato, I laugh, then tell her that's what Marty used to do. 'In our final days, I gave him

salad every mealtime. Salad with ham, salad with pork, and salad
with salad. That's all he deserved.'

'Didn't you love him?' asks Moira.

'I loved him once. He had an affair with his office boss,
Caroline… there was no going back.'

'But you loved him?'

I laugh again, jab one of my pieces of tomato. 'I never loved
him like I love Tracey, and I never loved Tracey as I love you. God, do
you think I'd be sitting here now if you'd have hightailed to London.
I'd have set up roadblocks on the A1 and the M1. You and I are
forever, girl. I'm sorry I gave you salad.'

'This is strange,' says Moira.

'It's so quiet.'

'The house feels colder.'

'The seats look empty,' I say glancing to the room.

'And what about Lizzie? asks Moira with a little hesitation.
'Do you love her too?'

I look up, raise my eyebrows… 'Do I love Lizzie? Short
answer, no. The longer answer, it would be nice to have feelings for
Lizzie that were more than just pity and physical attraction. She's a
beautiful girl, but to be honest, I've failed to get to the bottom of her.
It's a good thing that she seems attached to Tracey – I'm happy that
Tracey's taken Lizzie with her. I don't think we'd have become the
perfect threesome had she stayed here.'

'Because of the fire? Because she's still capable of causing
harm?' says Moira.

'I don't think Lizzie started the fire that killed her parents. If
you ask me, and it's only my opinion, I think Lizzie bears guilt that is
not hers. Kids often blame themselves for parental misfortune.
Lizzie just seems to believe that one day she had parents and the

next day they were gone – and she's to blame. I reckon if Tracey shows her love she'll flourish, and then maybe we can all love her.'

'You've reformed Lizzie,' murmurs Moira. 'You changed me too.'

I slap her hand on the table and joke, 'It wasn't me who dyed your hair and made you super-gorgeous.'

'If Lizzie was a wild girl, then I was a shy girl. You gave both of us everything we have.'

I force the piece of tomato on my fork between Moira's lips, smile, then tell her that what my three girls have given me is far, far more than I've ever given them. I'm no longer making salads every evening for a guy who fell for a fat ugly woman who had a hedgehog nesting at the top of her legs.

Bed-hopping

Not since Marty left and I first got to know Tracey intimately has circumstance provided such an opportunity to indulge in everlasting sex. Moira and I are free to go to bed and begin making love on Saturday evening and carry on unrelenting until we drop to sleep on Sunday night. We know it is possible, all that is required is a willingness to commence.

We climb the stairs, view the three bedrooms from the landing before deciding to lay on Lizzie's bed. There are five or six dildos strewn on the carpet and other sex toys and appliances tucked under the pillows. The girls have enjoyed themselves before leaving; now we understood why they made so much noise.

We lay there, sniffing the duvet, discovering long hairs from Lizzie's ponytail, and finding tiny smears on the linen. We squirt perfumes at the bedside to create the scent of their bodies and say aloud, 'Miss you Tracey, miss you Lizzie.'

We lay on our sides, face to face, swap kisses, run our fingers through each other's hair, and once or twice venture to the other's neck. Words were few, feelings of intense love are plentiful and for more than half an hour it is enough to gaze into the other's soul.

We swap beds, go to Moira's. She turns on her laptop and begins to show me the progress she's made on our porn movie. And its opening scene is promising – Tracey removing Lizzie's knickers with her teeth, but from thereon it seems all downhill. Shaky hands, poor camera direction, flashes of skin, flashes of the fireplace and the ceiling, Katy hiding her face, and the highlight of me shielding Moira from wandering hands. We've produced a failure – another memory of six folks being silly. 'There's two of us left,' says Moira as she closes the laptop lid.

We kiss some more then Moira lays with her head on my breasts while I twiddle her hair and attempt to convince her she is the most beautiful girl in the world. We are warm and content. We mention sex, but what's the rush. We think of all the places in the house where we haven't screwed before, and when Moira suggests the loft we laughed and say we must buy some ladders to reach the trapdoor.

It sounds corny, I know, but over and over we hum 'I love you' and again and again we hug and lose our dreams in each other's eyes. Then we kiss more passionately and I begin to notice Moira's lips reddening. I say we'll have more room in my bed. 'For what?' she murmurs. I lift her chin and rub her forehead with my nose.

We saunter from Moira's bed to the landing. I point to space where Tracey's suitcase has been. 'She'll be so busy working, she won't have time for sex,' I say. Then I hold Moira against the railing, place my hands under her top and press my hips against hers. And we kind of explode in a moment of instant lust. Our hands heave at each other's clothes as they fall down our bodies and noose over our heads. Our flesh fuses but our tops remain fast on our faces and our arms chaotically flail in the air. We topple over because our skirts cuff our ankles. We hear my phone ringing downstairs, and both of us shout 'It's Tracey'. Somehow Moira escapes, then leaps down the steps with one arm and her neck trapped in her top. I see her dart into the room, seconds later she yells, 'It's Tracey.' I shake off my bindings then jump down the stairway in four daring strides. Moira hands me the phone and I scold Tracey for leaving me.

Tracey sobs then manages to say, 'I couldn't tell you. How could I say 'goodbye' when it's not 'goodbye' – it would have killed me. I'm sorry, Rosa. I'll be back – I promise you that I'll be back.'

Tears splash on the phone's body and I'm blubbering uncontrollably. 'You got there okay?' I blubber. Through the opening minutes, we talk nonsense, mention Lizzie and Moira, stupid things like the weather outside, and which vases I've used for the flowers. Tracey tells me that they're in a posh hotel room with a bed as big as a football field. She intends to work 14 hours a day so they can be back before the end of the summer. Moira knows how to manage the café finances. Moira knows all the wholesalers. Moira had better take good care of me and ensure I have a constant supply of gin. Lizzie is fascinated with London and wants to visit Buckingham Palace and the Tower. They haven't eaten since this morning because their bellies are in their boots. We cry some more, then Moira speaks to Lizzie and we all scream 'I'm missing you' ten times a second. They'll call tomorrow – if we're screwing, they'll call again. Everyone loves everyone and by the time the conversation ends the phone is drowned in tears. I hug Moira and we rejoice that we haven't been forgotten.

Then comes the ice-breaker (as if we needed one!), we suddenly realize we're standing a foot from the single-paned front window – naked – and the old guy who walks his dog three times a day is gawping with his false teeth hovering between his withered lips on the pavement outside. We shake our tits to give him a thrill, then run off to the kitchen. We determine to screw each other senseless in the garden, on the kitchen table, on the sofa, on the rug, on the stairs, in Moira's bed, on the landing, in Lizzie's bed, and finally in my bed with one of us being strapped securely for the other to relish, and if that takes all night, so be it... Moira complains, 'We'll take turns with the bondage – that's fair!'

'You are beautiful,' I say.

'And so are you,' says Moira.

A rare invitation

We did it. We expended every last drop of energy on every available surface; we set a new record for sex in different places, even daring to test the solidity of the work surface in the kitchen and climbing atop of the wardrobe, which I must say proved unsteady. By two in the morning, Moira could take no more, but that didn't stop us laughing at our achievement nor from getting up in the middle of the night to binge on bread rolls, biscuits, and cakes.

Surprisingly, by 10..30 Sunday morning, we were dressed, reinvigorated, and heading up the street to pop in on Katy. We took a detour along by my parents' house, and Moira nagged me to call – I haven't been in months, my life is too complicated to explain.

I knock, enter tentatively, and when father catches a glimpse of my face he cries, 'Good God, look what the wind's blown in!'

Mother frowns, then sees Moira. 'She's another one in tow,'
she tells father.

Father twists in his chair, 'And who's this?'

"Moira,' I say.

'Wasn't the last one named Moira?' says mother.

'It's the same Moira – she's dyed her hair.'

Father scrunches his eyes. 'My word, she's a bit of a looker.'
He looks Moira up and down, nods in approval and tells mother to
bring a stool from the kitchen for Moira to sit on. I, of course, get the
piano stool next to the sideboard.

As mother brings in the stool, she examines Moira and
appears somewhat aghast. 'You're the same Moira as before?'

'I am,' says Moira.

'You're a fine-looking girl to be with Our Rosa,' says mother.

Moira smiles in embarrassment. I tell father to stop ogling
her. 'She's an improvement on Tracey Cummings,' he says.

'Tracey and Lizzie have gone to London,' I say. 'On
business...'

'I can imagine,' says mother insinuating they've gone
whoring.

'Katy tells us you've still got that café,' adds father. 'And who
the hell is Lizzie?'

And then for half an hour, I fill them in on some details of the
past months. They are confused about relationships – how can I love
Moira and Tracey at the same time; what's wrong with Lizzie – is she
ugly? Isn't she one of your kind? Father professes to know that
lesbians come in all shapes and sizes. I should stick with 'this one' on
the stool from the kitchen. And when I get to tell them of the MAID
MOIRA'S expansion, the Headingley branch, the city branch, those in
Sheffield and Wakefield, well, both my parents are flabbergasted.
Their eyeballs are bouncing on their knees when I inform them that

we've sold 85% of the business to a London millionaire who is planning to open branches of MAID MOIRA'S in the country's capital. I leave them in no doubt that this brilliant achievement is down to Tracey's business flair and she's now the most demanded former whore in the British Isles. It is ascribable to Tracey's genius that very soon their worthless second daughter is going to be rich, not just physically, but monetarily too!

'Tracey Bloody Cummings... well I never,' gasps father.

'It takes some believing,' says mother. She crooks her finger at Moira and adds, 'Are you sure it's not down to that girl – she must have brains. She looks intelligent.' They were so impressed with my new blonde lover that we got invited for Sunday dinner. And when mother extracted from Moira the news that she had no parents and had spent her childhood in an orphanage, my parents were likely thinking of adoption forms and buying a third armchair for the room. They told her she's pretty a dozen more times. They told her they'd always wanted a daughter like her – Katy is far too lanky and I went off the rails years ago – 'Doesn't Moira know about the film?' asked father referring to my gang-bang at the Golf Club.

I joke and say that Moira wishes she'd starred in the film. Moira goes bright red. Mother tells her she looks even more stunning with a bit of color in her cheeks.

We eat dinner from trays and wash the dishes like a pair of caring daughters. We are ordered to call again. They wish to see more of my sweet little virgin... and so do I.

Simple Stories (part two)

By late afternoon, we're once again in my bed. I'm naked, accepting thrills from Moira's hand and the white vibrator that's shaped like a microphone. She's so gentle with me and builds the sensations as if she's stacking playing cards, and I moan softly as we gaze into each other's eyes.

Occasionally Moira asks if I want her to do something else; she kisses my belly or licks my nipples. I tell her that she's wonderful, I could lay here for the next month, there's no rush to climax and the day is yet young. She's so astonishingly beautiful I never tire of staring at her face and still find it hard to believe how dying her hair has increased her appeal, not that she can be more appealing than she is. If I were able to screw her forever then I'd say it's too brief, and when she screws me, forever seems like only a second of intense pleasure. Between moans, I tell Moira how much I love her and how there just being the two of us, knowing there'll be no interruption, causes every thrill to be more precious than all the thrills I've ever experienced. She runs her fingers delicately over my pussy and smiles angelically as she lays the vibrator precisely on my flesh. And then she straightens her back so the outline of her small tits fills the space beneath her top. One simple movement but it's so erotic; I take hold of the vibrator and ask Moira to take off her clothes. It's as if I haven't seen her naked in a hundred years and if I don't see her body I'll die immediately.

Moira takes the vibrator from me, lays it at my side, then lifts each of my knees so they're wider apart and an inch or two off the mattress. She pokes me for a while and runs her tongue on her lower lip. There are no words just the obvious physical statement of what she's about to do. And when she sees my thighs tremble and my hands flatten on the bedsheet, she slides her skirt and pants off her ass before raising her top and then teasing me by playing with her bra. 'Do it,' I plead. She removes her bra ever so slowly and the moment I glimpse her erect nipples I feel my pussy pulsate and my entire body tingle. Our eyes are fixed as she goes down on me, and that first lick is akin to the first orgasm of life – so perfectly aimed, so deliciously lasting and smooth that I almost scream in ecstasy. And Moira arouses me as if the timing and the circumstance of today is the ideal setting for ultimate arousal. She guides me to sublime heights, she gives me feelings that compare with any from my past and gifts me pleasures that are beyond description. Our eyes do not blink even when I'm shaking, shuddering, and releasing the blissful liquid of climax. For minutes, and minutes more I stutter through rare magnificence and feel my body tense and spasm and give its all to my fabulous untrained lover. And when I fall back and Moira climbs to my face to share the taste of her lips, I know without a doubt I'm the luckiest girl alive.

We sigh, we kiss, and then Moira props her head on her wrists, hovering over my face, a picture of incredible splendor. 'Doesn't Moira know about the film?' she says repeating my father's words. 'I do know. Sometimes, I've imagined what you looked like with all those folks screwing you. I imagined it then... that's why I was so good... I was determined to make you cum.'

I tell her that she always pleases me. She knows how to turn me on and no lover in the past compares with her. She's special; sex couldn't be better. I love her so much my heart is bursting. But Moira wants to speak. She tells me that she isn't sure what she needs to say but she must have the opportunity to explain. She's wanted to talk since she fixed her banner to the room wall. I must listen, and when I've listened, we'll have more sex, and the sex will be amazing because I'll know what's going on in her head.

'You've so much more experienced than me,' she begins, 'and there are times when I feel inadequate…'

'Don't be silly.' She tells me to keep quiet. I must allow her to ramble.

'I know about the Golf Club and the barroom, and I know how all the girls in the cages earned their money. I know you've had lovers, many lovers, and your memories are greater than mine. So, sometimes I think what's so special about me – nothing is special. I'm a girl who's had sex with you and Tracey, and once with Lizzie. When we're making love, I don't know if I'm doing everything you want from me. I know so little, I'm a beginner who has much to learn.'

'You are fabulous,' I say.

'Don't interrupt,' says Moira. She falls on her back and looks to the ceiling. 'That Saturday evening… simple stories are the best… yes, I planned to get us back together and end all the misery you were going through. I couldn't bear you being frustrated – you love sex. It was cruel what we did to you. I wanted things to return to normal, and that's why I tied those poles to my ankles and wrists. You could have sex with me, all five of you, and then we'd be happy again. But Rosa…' Moira takes a deep breath and seems to pluck up the courage to continue. 'But I had another motive – a selfish motive. Deep down, I wanted my body to feel what it was like to have sex with five people. I longed to know how you felt being gang-banged, for if I knew that, I could screw you on equal terms, I wouldn't be disadvantaged by my inexperience. Don't get me wrong, I don't pine for sex, I long for the knowledge of what it feels like so I may understand what you see in me. Sure, that Saturday evening, as you put it, I chickened out. I called you 'Mum' and you immediately recognized my fears. But my fears, Rosa, weren't to do with having five folks screwing my body, they were to do with the familiarity of

those touching me. If five strangers had been screwing me, then I'd
have called you Rosa instead of Mum. Can't you understand my
curiosity? I don't know what it's like feeling one dick inside me. I
often think when we're having sex, why you should want me when
I've so little to offer – I've even thought that you pity me because I'm
an orphan and my sexual attraction is something of a myth. And
another thing that goes through my head is the idea of you watching
me have sex with a group of strangers – maybe I turned you on just
now, but I'm certain that if you saw me acting like a little whore –
just once – you'd not only appreciate me more, but you'd lock the
scene in your mind forever and perhaps recall it when we make love.
You'd see me as a woman. You'd respect me because I'd done
something you've done. I'd be different because you'd know what
I'd done. Yes, I've imagined what you did with the punters at SMA
and I'm not asking you to imagine anything. If I ever get screwed by
strangers, I'd want you to be there; it's important that you'd be there
so I can prove that I am capable of pleasing you in any way you may
wish. In short, it's about me feeling worthy. Sex with men doesn't
bother me. Somehow, someway, I just need to feel I deserve all that
you lavish on me, and then I won't be scared of disappointing you.'

'You're crazy,' I say. 'To me, you are Moira – my perfect
lover, my other half.'

'But I don't feel half,' she says. 'I need to feel worthy of you.'

And what's my answer? Perhaps I run away from what she
has said, and I climb over her and start making love to her, I start
screwing her like I'm one of those strangers she mentions, I pour
over her body like I'm trying to prove that our sex can't be improved
on – lay back my sweet little virgin and let me take your body to
higher realms.

Trying to understand

Over the next few days, Moira lets me know that I haven't understood her feelings. She insists that it's not about having sex for the sake of having sex, it's about knowing what it's like to have group sex. She seems to believe that I saved her from Katy, Marty, Tracey, and Lizzie because I thought she couldn't endure such an orgy. In my mind she's fragile and I sought to preserve her innocence. We contradict each other, there are misunderstandings, she comes out with statements that don't make sense, and I suppose, so do I. I tell her in detail what it's like to be used as a piece of meat and how degrading it can be when guys are screwing your ass and you can't do a damn thing about it if you're suddenly revolted. The pleasure can be minuscule and the pain enormous. Shame is free, sometimes your self-worth disintegrates completely.

Moira always comes back with, 'It's not about sex – it's about you knowing I've done what you've done.'

One afternoon we have something of an argument. I suggest I get in touch with Angela and ask if she'll put Moira in the cages for a couple of nights. She tells me to forget everything she's ever said about strangers but I point out that if I do forget, she won't forget. Yes, we endure awkward hours before I persuade her to go to bed for yet another sex session. I think I'll eventually get her to believe that me giving her orgasms, and her giving me orgasms is the only matter worthy of consideration.

But then we arrive at Wednesday morning in the café. We've had a phone call from Tracey and spoken with Lizzie too. By the end of the call, Moira and I are talking about the foursome we had on the evening before the girls went to London. We exchange memories of what Lizzie did to Tracey or what I did to Moira and I'm surprised over the details Moira can pluck from her mind. Before we set off home Moira tells me this conversation is not dead – we'll resume over coffee and a sandwich at the kitchen table.

She kept her word. She made the coffee and the sandwich. By 1.15 we're sitting on the chairs and Moira is wearing the cheekiest grin I've seen on her lips. I tell her that after we've eaten, I'll take her upstairs and fix those wired suckers to the machine and her body and I won't be patient before turning the dial up to 10. She laughs and brings up the last description she made at the café and informs me that she has a method in her madness by talking about our four-girl sexual adventure.

Moira tells me that she sneakily watched me throughout the foursome. She recounts what each of us did, where I stood or laid in proximity to her, whose body parts I touched and what kind of expression nested on my face. She remembers everything to the finest detail. 'You were horny,' she said,' but you were about to get even hornier.'

'When we set about Lizzie?' I said.

Moira leans toward me, 'Truth or lie?'

'Truth,' I said not knowing where she's leading me.

'My face came down Lizzie's body, I'm looking sideways, watching you watching me, and as I cupped my hands under Lizzie's knees, I saw you quiver, and when I licked her… God, Rosa, you were trickling.'

Strangely, I felt guilty. Grudgingly, I said, 'True.'

'And a little after, when I rode up Lizzie's body and squat on her face, you were oozing – no-one was touching you but you were having an orgasm. I did it to turn you on. I knew you wanted to see Lizzie's tongue inside me – didn't you?'

'Oh, God, let's go upstairs,' I yelled snatching Moira's hand. Moira pulled her hand away.

'How many times has that happened before?'

'Never,' I said.

'What would you go through seeing me being screwed by a few guys? Wouldn't that blow your mind – truth or lie?'

'Truth... you know it's the truth, Moira, but how could I...?'

'Whose choice is it?'

'Your choice.'

'Would you abandon me?'

'Never – I love you.'

'You don't care that you'd lose your sweet little virgin?'

'Yes, I do.'

'You'd be jealous?'

'Yes.'

'But you'd let me do it?'

'Yes. I couldn't stop you.'

'And would it be worth it to watch me being screwed?'

'Moira... what's happened? Why are you doing this to me?'

She rose from her seat and began to clear the table, rushing, glancing at me as if I must show the intensity of my desires. She's as high as a kite, twirling her hair and behaving like someone with neurosis. I tell her to calm down, she has nothing to prove. 'What's gotten into you?'

When the table is clear, she stands next to me, takes my hand, and pushes it under her top. I fondle her tits believing that's what she's asking of me. Then she puts my other hand down her pants and places her fingers over mine as she steers them into her pussy. I'm confused. Is this Moira? She's behaving out of character and I can't find a word to say.

I think that by poking her she'll suddenly revert to normal, but she stands wearing a crazy look and dangles her hair on my face. She takes off her top and bra and hangs them around my neck. Next, her skirt falls, then her knickers, and she asks if I like her body. She knows I like her body – I adore her.

Moira releases my fingers, places herself between me and the table edge, then leans back with the skirt and bra held tightly in her hands and pulling my face to her pussy. 'Lick it,' she demands. 'Am I so desirable, Rosa Saint John?'

I do my duty but is this duty or is Moira off her head. I don't think she's ever called me Rosa Saint John. She's certainly never been so tartish, or so falsely bossy. She heaves on the skirt and bra on my neck, raises her hips, and smothers my face so I can barely breathe. I can't lick her, I chew her, I attempt to defy her efforts to be brutal but all the while I search for a reason why this is happening. My sweet girl behaves like a monster because she claims to have the urge to be screwed by strangers. I force her legs apart and trap her thighs in my arms, and when the skirt and bra slip off my head, I gain control and manage to deliver sexual pleasure. Moira accepts defeat and gradually becomes submissive. When she relaxes, I become gentle with her, find relief when her groans are filling the kitchen with pleasure, and feel pleased that my sweet little virgin is returning to me. After fifteen minutes or so, I pull her toward me so her legs are around my waist. I carry her upstairs and lay her on my bed, then find the strap-on and affix a dildo in the mold of a penis. I screw her on her back, place her in a doggy position and screw her more, and repeat the process until Moira is fully pleasured and her body is telling me that she's had enough. And when we lay side by side when it's over, I show Moira the dildo. 'That's what a dick feels like,' I say. She cuddles up to me, snuggles her face into my tits and I feel tears drip onto my cleavage.

A spoonful of turmoil

Moira's mood fluctuates, not wildly but enough to be disconcerting. This morning at the café she blared, 'Fucking hell' when she dropped an egg on the floor. Moira seldom curses – there's anger hiding in her head.

I occasionally see her staring at an object; a minute passes and she's okay again. She hasn't referred to the weird conversation about having sex with strangers but I feel sure those thoughts are swilling in her mind and I wonder if they're ever going to disappear. I'm being extra nice to her and trying to allay those feelings she has of being inadequate. I tell her she's sexy, tell her that I think of her body awake or asleep and that my heart pounds with love-beats even when I'm sitting on the toilet. I shout 'Gorgeous' or 'Give me a smile' when I go to the kitchen and she's in the room. I get her to flash her legs or push her top off one shoulder to show me a piece of her flesh.

Don't get me wrong, she's still the fabulous Moira and most of the time she's as sweet as candy. It occurs to me that she's missing Tracey and Lizzie. Perhaps an often silent house seems strange to her. It's not impossible to believe that she enjoyed our foursome so much that she longs for another to happen when the girls get back from London.

After getting home from the café we sit for a while on the sofa and scoff half a box of those chocolates left by the girls. I make a display of sucking the chocolate and suggest taking Moira upstairs for sex. I hold a chocolate in the air and tell her it could be her pussy. She giggles. I suggest other things and this leads to me going on about the penis-shaped dildo – how did she find it? did it feel different from the other dildos? shall I go get it and screw Moira on the sofa while she eats the other half of the chocolate selection?

Moira tells me she intended to play a game on her laptop. I say we should review our second-rate porn movie. She prefers the game. I fake being angry and scald her for deserting me in favor of a keyboard, or control pad, or whatever it's called that she manipulates in her hands.

Moira goes upstairs. I pop another chocolate in my mouth then lie on the sofa with a cushion under my neck. I intend to have a nap, but that's not what happens.

A few minutes pass before I'm in fantasy mode. Moira had mentioned 'the idea of you watching me have sex with a group of strangers.' Her words from her lips. I suddenly thought of Joe and started fantasizing about calling him and asking him how much money he'd pay for a sweet little virgin and would he and his mates be interested. He's bound to be interested – send him a photo of Moira with a note declaring that this girl is longing for dicks and you're free to screw her anyhow, any place, and for as long as you like. Jealousy fades in fantasies, all folks do is get off on imagined images, and I'm no exception.

I get a picture of that hotel room where I endured an eight hour (or more) gang-bang with Joe and his mates and visualize Moira and I waltzing through the doorway. There are four or five guys assembled around a large empty bed, mouths frothing, muscles rippling on naked bodies, and dicks so erect they aim at the ceiling. I push Moira in the small of the back, she stumbles forward, hands grab her and so easily toss her onto the white uncreased bedsheet. Before I've introduced her, they're ripping off her clothes and clawing at her points of access. Moira screams and she's slapped instantly. They manhandle her, stretch her limbs and violate her with their hands. Some guy at her head rams his dick in her mouth, another guy starts screwing her and I begin fingering myself as I creep closer for a better view. Moira's yelling for me but I encourage the guys to abuse her – 'she wants fucking, not tickling,' I scream. I get a picture of Moira's terrified face as more dicks crave for oral sex; she's covered in white runny liquid, licking it, swallowing it, gurgling for breath. Then they turn her and the guy beneath her thrusts upward to her pussy and another guy's pounding her ass. She cries 'Help me,' but I'm lost in a string of orgasms and just wanting the guys to be more brutal. They turn her upside down, gobble her, invade her without mercy, then they trap her in a sandwich and screw her standing, her feet off the floor, her body almost lifeless and her head flopping in utter defeat. I'm so turned on that I cling to the thrill of Moira's pain and realize that my hand is down my pants and it's only a pleasant fantasy.

I roll off the sofa, run up the stairs and take Moira's laptop from her knees, 'Pretend I'm a stranger, I've come to rape you,' I howl. She looks startled but mildly amused. I tear off her clothes, then tear off my clothes, and before she can think of a word to say, I'm screwing her, devouring her body disgustingly and the only thing she says is that she was in the middle of a game. Oh God, sex is superb and Moira fully co-operates. And when it's over, I tell Moira I've been fantasizing over her – the fantasy wasn't enough, I had to have her.

'Why the stranger?' she says.

'I thought you may like it that way.'

A reality assessment

I'm becoming obsessive; the more I think about Moira's moods the more I come to believe they're an invention I've created. Moira's moods don't swing – I look at her from every angle and my mind tosses up conflicting impressions of her.

I'm obsessed with her body. It's like the old days when Tracey and I spent more hours screwing than getting on with life. Some mornings I screw Moira on the counter or a table after the café closes. She takes me home in the van (yes, I've screwed her in the back of the van) and I screw her on the kitchen table. I screw her in bed in the afternoon. I screw her mid-evening and screw her again before we go to sleep. There's something inside me that says if I screw her often enough, she'll forget about strangers, forget about dicks, and she'll become my everlasting love. She'll be satisfied. She won't feel inadequate. Neither of us will ever, ever, ever wish for sex with another partner.

We bind each other to the bed, to the railings on the landing, to anywhere where straps can be circled. We discuss what to do next. We've fertile imaginations and we've created lots of new ways to have orgasms.

But here is the stumbling block: my fantasies get more frequent, 50% of my brain is convinced that Moira's desire for strangers with stiffened dicks is real. That former plea of hers to be ravished and humiliated still exists. When I'm pleasing her, I often wonder if she's wishing I'm a guy who doesn't give a damn if she lives or dies.

I've been seconds away from asking her if she'd like me to arrange a gang-bang with Joe and his mates. I argue with myself that I'd love to see her being seriously molested, then refused to believe I could bear such a sight. I'd lose my sweet little virgin to a fantasy. I'd forever regret trading her innocence for a lecherous memory. I'd end up losing the most precious love of my life. But watching her being screwed would be exquisitely beautiful. Oh hell, what can I say to Moira to halt the suffering?

She hasn't mentioned strangers lately. She doesn't complain when I lift her top or unexpectedly sneak behind her and lean her forward over the sofa or someplace else. I'll come downstairs naked, not ask, but just fondle her body and have sex with her. She can be in the shower and I'll have sex with her. She's playing a game and I dive under her duvet and have sex with her. If I were a guy, she'd be having babies every few hours.

One day I had a brief conversation with Tracey about my behavior. Tracey said I shouldn't worry; if Moira is dissatisfied, she'll let me know. 'Moira is your sweet little virgin, and that won't change, no way,' professed Tracey, but Tracey doesn't know that Moira once spoke about strangers as if they'd make her feel like a sexual equal.

One evening, and I'm not sure if Moira was just messing with my thoughts or being serious, she's screwing me with the penis-like dildo when she blurts out, 'This is so like a real dick that the veins seem to pulsate when I drive into you.' I kind of froze and got myself wallowing in jealousy as I imagined that she secretly yearned to be handling a real dick and craved for it to be inside her. Perhaps it is Moira who's not content – maybe she too has fantasies and they're always simmering on the surface, but she doesn't tell me.

The way forward

I'm likely coming across as someone half-demented. If loving Tracey in the early days proved painful, then hell, I'm in the grip of full-time torture. Not only do I love Moira, but she occupies my thoughts so profoundly that averting my eyes from her face or body seems like a crime. I keep burning my hand on the hot plate, bumping into objects, tripping over, failing to hear the words when a customer speaks, gazing at her and forgetting what I'm doing, and just uttering her name for no apparent reason. I called a huge guy with a long

beard and arms as long as streetlamps Moira. Another guy asked me
the time, and I said, Moira. Moira thinks it's funny but she doesn't
realize that I'm seriously love-struck — not to this extent, anyway.

And it's not simply a case of out-of-control love. If I lose sight
of her for a few seconds, well, that can be rectified. I move, think,
thank God, she's not disappeared. She laughs and waves her hand
and tells me she's going nowhere. Then we exchange blown kisses
and comfort is restored.

But a far worse problem than this is the sexual chemistry that
exists between us. Because I never take my eyes off her, I see every
movement of her body and notice every tiny exposure of flesh. She'll
move her head and I'll see a part of her neck usually covered. She'll
lean forward and reveal a small fraction more of her tits. She'll walk,
and her skirt hem shifts — I thirst on a blob of thigh or on that super-
exciting sight that is the rear of her knees. I get turned on five times
a minute, and every turn-on fills me with a desire to molest her body.
When there are folks about, I can't lift her skirt or fold her top from
her shoulders even though I'm buzzing with the desire to have sex.

I have a permanent damp patch in my knickers and my belly
resembles a cement-mixer. My thighs could illuminate a light bulb
and my nipples are visible beneath my uniform. What must
customers think when they see a girl serving whose lips look like
she's being screwed from behind? I tremble holding sausage
sandwiches. I spill coffee onto saucers. I can transform breakfast on
a plate into some part of Moira's body and get the female equivalent
of an enormous erection.

This morning reminded me of the time when Marty took two
or three of those little blue pills and his dick stayed erect long after
both of us were satisfied. If customers occupied tables and Moira
and I found a free minute or two behind the counter, I'd fall to my
knees and play with her while concealing myself under the recess. I'd

remove her knickers, and once when customers were chatting loudly, I was slurping on her pussy as two guys were ordering. Gee… how erotic is that? Quite honestly, I thought of taking Moira to the center table and screwing her before an appreciative audience.

I shut the café at 12.10 and laid Moira on the freezer. I lift all her clothes to her neck and poked her so much that the frozen items below her likely melted. Moira said we should go have sex in the van but we had sex on the front seat because the van was parked a good distance from other vehicles. Half an hour later we're performing 69s on the sofa in our room. I screw her while she's laying upside down on the stairs, then she screws me on the top step, then we go to my bed and the sex becomes so ravenous that we're filling East Leeds with screams as loud as roars from tigers.

A ten-minute break and then we're having sex on the kitchen table again. After this Moira screws me on the garden bench, and we don't stop when rain falls, and we roll naked on the wet lawn until traces of mud on our skin force us to come inside.

It's obscene! I'm obscene. Rosa's confessions are obscene but I swore, in the beginning, to be as truthful as I dare to be. And I've got to confess it got even worse than this. After we'd eaten our meal at around 5.45, I took Moira upstairs again and this time tied her limbs to the four corners of the bed. Yes, she consented to more sex. Yes, she allowed me to do whatever I wished. I was as horny as I'd been this morning and I promised Moira I'd give her multiple orgasms or however many is possible.

I gag her, blindfold her, and then get to work on her body. At first, she's responding and raising her hips to meet the dildos. She's letting out sounds of pleasure and willing me to be as adventurous as I can. At some point, I go easy on her and slide in the dildos slowly. I suck her skin, lavish attention on her neck, her tits, her belly, and her thighs, then decide I'll crawl up to her face and sit astride her mouth.

I'm gentle, I take off her gag and she doesn't move. I push the blindfold onto her forehead. Hell, Moira is sound asleep. She looks beautiful. Something tells me to get out of bed to admire her bound in nakedness. I'm incredibly turned on – after all this, hot, wet, and seeped in fabulous sensations.

I stand at the side of the bed and that fantasy of seeing Moira being screwed by a bunch of guys with ten-inch dicks suddenly begins playing out in my mind. Oh God, I dwell on every part of her, imagine what guys may do to her especially knowing she's a virgin. I'm not going to say what I do next but the image of Moira being gang-banged gets stronger and stronger. I swear that if she desires to experience such an ordeal, I'll arrange it, I'll accompany her. The notion of my fantasy meeting reality is just too tempting to resist.

Wondering what will come next

Almost daily, we speak with Tracey and Lizzie. Tracey tells us what she's been doing regarding the progress of MAID MOIRA'S outlets and Lizzie says how her fascination with London never wanes. We tell the girls about our amazing sex-life and they complain that they haven't too much free time to spend in bed. During one conversation between Moira and our absent lovers, I'm screwing Moira with the strap on and she interjects every phrase with an extended moan or a 'God almighty'. She slavers over the phone screen while the girls encourage me to screw her harder. Tracey and Lizzie are getting along magnificently and I get the impression that their bond is strengthening.

Our bond is faultless, and if love were contagious, we'd have contaminated most of the folks in Northern England. Sex would be as common as breathing and scientists throughout the world would be searching for a vaccine.

Did we ease off or temper our activities – no way! When outside temperatures soared, we went to open-air locations where screwing could be enacted without the threat of arrest. I took Moira to the roof of the tower block and leaned her over the perimeter wall so she could merrily gaze over Leeds while her ass was being merrily serviced. She loved it and joked it was 'the high point of her life'.

That same day we had sex in the bushes at the park; folks passed on the nearby path and had no idea why the leaves were rustling.

We took several sex toys to the lane beyond the woods, where Marty once took me in his car but resisted screwing me for some pathetic reason that I forget. Moira tied me to a tree and had me hooting more frequently than those owls in the barn on the farmer's field. She pretended to drive off half-way through, and the second session proved even more exciting than the first.

We had sex on the riverbank beneath an azure sky in the red-hot sunshine. Moira got sunburned and the only cream we had came from her pussy. She had so many orgasms that the river level rose by a couple of inches. I've got to say that we dressed and undressed perhaps eight times; each time we decided to leave we changed our minds and had sex again, in a different place or a different position and once on a giant boulder some way into the woods.

Our most daring romp, though it lasted only a minute or two, came one night when we couldn't sleep because the air in the bedroom was so clammy. We came downstairs, both naked as usual. Some mad idea caused me to open the front door so we could feel colder air on our bodies. In a flash, I grabbed Moira's arm and dragged her to the middle of the road, and there I laid her on the road and had sex with her in the light of the streetlamps when everyone was sleeping but the local cats. We then ran inside and had a bout of hysterical laughter.

We had sex in the church grounds, a brief grope leaning against that tree on the back lane where Tracey first had me, and a two-minute grope in the changing room at the clothes store. And in between all these adventures, our love-making in the café and our house never abated.

But at least four or five times a day that fantasy of seeing Moira have sex with strangers kept resurfacing. She never directly brought up the subject but she inadvertently reminded me by choosing the penis-like dildo as her favorite toy to fix to the strap-on. Many times, I got to within moments of asking her if she'd like to be gang-banged – I couldn't find the courage to speak out.

Time to strike?

It's been weeks since I called Joe; maybe he's thought of me, maybe he hasn't. And what's he going to think if I offer a virgin to be gang-banged? Who's the virgin? What does she look like? Virgins are delicate and she may not be fun to play with?

And if he's agreeable and shows enthusiasm, does Moira come free or with a considerable price tag? Hell, if I'm worth a couple of grand, then Moira's worth a damned lot more.

Phone Joe. Don't phone Joe. Consult Moira. Give Moira the surprise of her life.

I pace up and down my bedroom. I call myself a heartless bitch. I tell myself that if Moira's wish is fulfilled it won't make a difference when we're having sex. But if I have erotic images in my head when I'm screwing her, won't that heighten the excitement? I'll talk to her. No, maybe the surprise is the better option.

I shout to her from the landing. When she comes up the stairs, she wears that look on her face that states 'You're going to screw me again.' But it's not sex that's the first thought, my heart beats rapidly and I get intense pangs of love surging from my belly to my neck. 'You're so beautiful I could pass out,' I say.

Moira laughs, tells me to collapse and she'll screw me while I'm unconscious.

Seconds later and we're in the bedroom, smooching, rubbing our bodies against each other and she's trying to take off her clothes. When I look into her eyes, I feel privileged and know for sure that no girl is as fortunate as me. She's perfect 24/7. I adore her – she's without blemishes, like a living masterpiece that's newly stepped from a painting. And when she takes off her underwear and stands before me like an offering from the Gods, she points to my knees and tells me they're knocking. 'That's what you do to me,' I say.

She shows me her shaking hand, 'And that's what you do to me.'

My mind goes blank; thrills shoot from nowhere. We keep our hands at our sides and press our tits softly, mine a little higher than hers, let our hips meet in a blissful union, and feel the skin on our legs tingle in anticipation.

Moira glances at the large black dildo on the drawers. She turns her hand to my pussy, 'Would you like that? she murmurs. I don't answer. I let her take control. She lowers me onto the bed and raises my legs over my head, she turns me to trap my feet under her shins then picks up the huge dildo and sucks it. I'm staring up at her body. She shunts forward an inch or two until my face is below her pussy. We're both wet and ready for entry. 'Rosa…' she says.

'My sweet little virgin,' I say.

And she keeps repeating my name as she drives the black dildo inside me as I stroke my tongue on the inside of her thigh to taste the delicious juice from her body. I feel so honored, feel sublime, feel majestically calm as if I'm being carried to Heaven. She glides the dildo with expertise, gives my mouth space to lap with ease and we're so synchronized that our bodies become one mass of sustainable pleasure. She enters me, I enter her, in, out, absurd sensations, sweet examinations of inner flesh, sweet releases of glorious lust, sweet tastes of female secrets, sweet commodities that we share that are bringers of orgasms.

'Rosa…' she cries as I eat from her. 'Oh Rosa… Oh, Rosa.'

We screw like sex has no end. We milk our bodily resources as if they're limitless. Sex in this one position before we steer carefully to the next, and the next, and we are rewarded with accumulative climaxes.

When we settle in each other's arms and our noses are touching on the pillow, Moira wriggles as though something's digging into her side. She reaches down between our bodies and two seconds later she's holding the penis-shaped dildo above her head. 'I wondered where that had gone,' she says with a grin.

Without thinking, I reply, 'Wouldn't you like it to be a real dick?'

Open to misinterpretation

Moira chose not to answer my question; she deliberately fixed her expression like she didn't want me to know what she thought. Soon after, we went downstairs; she took her time making a coffee and I sat in Tracey's armchair wondering if I'd blundered or fired the starting gun for the race to get Moira to forfeit her virginity.

During the next hours, I expected her to elaborate. I willed her to chastise me or jump on my legs and say, 'I don't want one dick

– I want a dozen dicks, and you must be there to soak up the memory. I can't wait, Rosa… put any plans you have into action, and I won't chicken out.'

Hey, when folks want something to happen, they imagine the outcome. As I watched Moira float about the house, I kept wishing Joe and his mates were on their way here to fulfill an appointment. There'd be nothing more stimulating than seeing Moira gang-banged on the sofa before taken upstairs to my bedroom. And then I think I'd be jealous and perhaps blame Moira for betraying me. She'd change; she'd wish to share her body with strangers at every opportunity.

Wrongly, I repeated the mistake of thinking about everything from my point of view. For the remainder of the day, I tried to cajole a response from Moira. I mentioned dicks and the few pluses about having sex with males, but Moira didn't bite.

We had sex before going to sleep, but in retrospect, it was me chasing Moira after I'd seen her in the shower. I led Moira to Lizzie's bed saying we should screw there in homage to our distant lovers. I'd exaggerate if I claimed Moira became hot and passionate; she just laid beneath me while I took advantage of her delights.

Decision made

I was going loopy; I'd dwell on images of Moira at the mercy of a maze of many arms and minutes later feel guilty about forcing her to do something she didn't wish to do. There were periods too when I resented her because she hadn't made her desires clear – I gave her the chance to say something by depositing the penis-like dildo on the sofa and leaving it there for comment. And when she didn't pass comment, I thought that meant she fully understood where I was heading – 'Don't fret, my sweet little virgin, Rosa is going to deliver unto you the most awesome experience of your life.'

But first I needed to establish if Moira had gone cold on me after the feeble performance in Lizzie's bed. I purposely set out to screw her as many times in twenty-four hours as is physically possible, and I must say, the scheme went remarkably well.

We spend the whole of Sunday having sex on every square foot of surfaces in the house. I barely let up for fifteen consecutive minutes and from morning to evening we never once covered our bodies in more than a bathrobe. I expected Moira to complain or even to cry, 'Not again!' but each time I approached her she welcomed me with open arms. We took it in turns taking the lead and nothing got repeated and the sex didn't become boring.

The sex in the garden with the open windows in the house behind us proved particularly exciting. We saw a young couple watching us, and soon after they were joined by another woman whom I took to be the female's sister. We screwed in full view of the street at my room window and I even laid Moira horizontally over the kitchen sink and ran water over her body as I'm giving her pleasure.

With each change of location, I felt sure Moira would ask if this was to be the last. And when for the third time I used the sofa as our arena and had Moira balancing gymnastically over the back support while I assaulted her with the penis-like dildo she kind of looked down her body to approve of what I was using, and I took that look of approval as a 'yes' to my question of if she'd like the penis to be real. I said to her, 'Next time...' as though it were a promise of what's to come, and she fluttered her eyelashes and groaned appreciatively.

Before we retired to bed for the final time that day, I looked in my tiny jacket's pocket for Joe's business card. After all the deliberations over Moira's fate, I, at last, decided I'd call Joe tomorrow to ask how interested he'd be in hiring the most gorgeous girl in Britain to be a plaything for him and his mates for two or three hours. The card wasn't there – I'd have to search for it after we've finished at the café in the morning.

Anticipation

Do I sleep soundly like a girl who's had enough fabulous sex to last her a lifetime and whose body may take a year to recover? I scarcely nod off for more than an hour. The nervousness sets in after I convince myself that Moira's gangbang is best served as a surprise. I'll set it up, persuade Moira to accompany me to some hotel room for some dubious reason that she won't find overly suspicious, and deliver her to a dozen erect dicks that one by one or two by two will slip inside her virtuous body. She'll get the greatest surprise ever, and nevermore fantasize about being screwed by a group of strangers – Moira meets reality with a bang!

My nerves go haywire and it's a wonder she doesn't wake and ask me what's happening to my body. From time to time I stare at her face and visualize it contorting with pleasure. She'll love it. I'll be watching and storing each penetration in my mind to be recalled time and time again. At some time, this week, Moira is going to know the sensation of dicks inside her.

We rise early; my expression must give her a clue. 'What's wrong with you today?' she says. We go to the café. I'm touchy-feely and tell Moira I love her at least three times an hour. She plays with her hair more than usual, not good hygiene for a café worker, but who cares. She stands with her weight on one leg more than usual. 'You're sexy,' I say. 'Some guys would pay a fortune for a girl like you.'

I bite my lip – that's going a bit too far. Then accidentally I mention virgins and stumble my way out of Moira's questions. She can tell I'm not acting normally and I'm taking too many liberties by groping her ass in front of customers.

I get one major boost for my plan when out of the blue Moira says 'that dildo' is still on the sofa. I joke, 'If it were real, it would have walked away.' She giggles and asks if I ever stop thinking about sex and I accuse her of being worse than me – she mentioned the dildo first.

We have a kiss and a cuddle before going home and another kiss and cuddle in the van. She's certain what I'm going to do to her once we get through the doorway and requests a delay for a coffee. 'Request granted, I've something to do,' I say. Moira looks a tad disappointed, but when I inform her that it's connected to her, she just smiles and accepts it as a valid excuse.

The delay for a coffee becomes an extended delay as I first go upstairs and inspect pockets in the clothes I've worn since I last saw Joe's business card. After the pockets, I search my drawers including the cash tins, and between the bundles of cash I've stored in other places. It's not under the bed nor dropped behind the chest of drawers. I come downstairs and Moira's laid on the sofa sipping her coffee. I check the kitchen, all the cupboards, the cutlery drawer, and come up with nothing. Moira shouts to say she's poured me fresh orange juice – it's at the side of the refrigerator. If I keep her waiting much longer, she's going to turn on her laptop and play a game.

I'm curious but not alarmed; I do misplace things occasionally and know the card won't be far away. Moira lifts her leg in the air and swivels her foot, and that's her way of saying she's ready for action.

As I approach the sofa, Moira stands, puts her finger to her lips, then directs me to follow her upstairs. We go into Moira's bedroom. She's behaving mysteriously, taps my shoulder then pats her hand on the bottom of her bed. I'm momentarily puzzled; she has me laying on the mattress with my feet close to the headboard and my head is tilted over the near edge. She looks down on me as she removes her top and bra, then kneels on the carpet and slowly steers my top and bra over my head. Once more she signals for me to be silent. She massages my temple with the tips of her fingers, and when I'm relaxed, her tits run smoothly across my face with her nipples always keeping an inch clear of my mouth. We've never done this before and it's so calming that I find my eyelids growing heavy and my whole body settling into the mattress.

Then Moira impresses me with her inventiveness; she spends an age kissing, pecking, and sucking my neck; the thrills are unique, sexually arousing but with a distinctive flavor that is tasted by only the top third of my body. Sometimes she wanders to my shoulders and tits; she uses her tongue and teeth but always leading with her lips. So, so relaxing, so beautifully sensational, and gentle. My eyes close; she's free to roam, free to excite me with her ever-busy lips.

And the last sensations I remember are the thrills dancing in my neck. Yes, Moira's hands caressed my tits but it is the memory of what she brought to life in my neck that will shine forever. I dozed off during a glorious experience. My sweet little virgin has come a long, long way on her journey to womanhood.

Caution ahead

A combination of a largely sleepless night after a marathon sex session, and Moira's fabulous neck-kissing, left me exhausted. Apart from the odd fondle, and a few tame efforts to track down Joe's business card, the next hours passed uneventfully with me dozing off several times and going to bed early, around 9.45. I dreamed that Tracey and Lizzie were living on the roof of the house, and the only way Moira and I could see them was by climbing a ladder affixed to the door of the garden shed. Each time we stepped on the ladder's rungs, a howling gale stirred and we had to hurry back into the kitchen to take shelter. When I told Moira of the dream in the morning, she wore a very weird look and said, 'You can't always get what you want.' I found that a very strange comment.

A very strange shift

The thing about folks that never ceases to amaze me is their predictability. All of us have a small collection of moods and a greater collection of habits. From my parents to Katy and Marty, to my girls, it's always easy to guess how they're going to be or how they'll react in any given circumstance. A shift at the café with Moira usually goes like clockwork – I chase her half the morning and intermittently, she smiles and submits at suitable moments. But that wasn't the case this morning. Moira behaved like a primary school teacher, kind of humored me, gently chastised me if I got over-excited and said, 'There's a time and place for everything.'

She often glanced in a way that she's never glanced. I didn't know what to make of it and asked her if she'd got a special surprise for when we'd finished work. Again, a question without a response. Something was going on in Moira's head and I didn't know if it was good or bad. She remained inscrutable and I can't remember us kissing until just before closing time when we were leaning over the counter and waiting for the last customer to get up from a table and leave. When he did leave, Moira kissed my ear before working her way to my mouth. She said mysteriously, 'This afternoon, we'll talk.'

Lesson from an orphaned child

Coffee and a salad sandwich, a tidy-up of the downstairs, and more ideas of where to look for the business card that bear no fruit, then Moira orders me to sit in the armchair facing her on the sofa. It's time for our talk; she has a few things to say and she hopes that I don't mind listening.

'I'm not one of those people who has lots to say,' she begins, 'I guess it began early in my life. In a children's home, you keep your mouth shut, you don't want to stand out. I always thought that keeping a low profile is best. Oh, that's not to say that I didn't yearn for someone to talk with. Things would cross my mind, and as a child, I didn't have answers. Sometimes I'd cry under my bedsheets. Sometimes I felt ever so lonely. Sometimes the only thing I had left was crying. And you know what... if an attendant asked me why I was crying, I'd tell her that I'd stumbled and hurt my foot, or I'd bellyache, or headache. That fixed things. Those answers were answers attendants could deal with. I learned very quickly that it proved beneficial to survival not to get too close to an attendant. Get close, receive comfort, hear a kind word, and you think you've found a friend. Then the friend leaves, and you're back to square one. The loneliness comes stronger than before and your heart is already broken. So, I remained aloof. Politeness doesn't get you into bother and knowing that you're just one of many kids without parents doesn't make you feel that you are victimized. I got on with it knowing someday my time at the orphanage will end and if it gets replaced by living on my own, well, I won't lose anything, I'll be the same, except in different surroundings. Rosa, you've got parents, a sister too, so you can't understand what it's like to be isolated. Even bad parents or hostile siblings are focusses of attention – I had a rag doll, and even that was torn to shreds by a boy who threw a tantrum.'

'I'm not pitying myself by telling you this, it's just how it was, nobody's fault, just how my life evolved. Some folks are born lucky and some folks reap misfortune; that's how the world works and that's what makes us all so different.'

'Hey, Tracey never talks about having any family and Lizzie's only got her uncle, so it's not just me who's not privileged. There are millions of folks who are born to suffer in one way or another, and there's no use complaining. You get on with it and believe that the sun may shine tomorrow.'

'I left the orphanage. Sure, I felt pleased to go – no more promises of adoption, no more pretending I'm not hurting inside, no more temptations to think that one of the attendants will think I'm special and then take me home with them. I got that unhealthy room with the damp wallpaper and the smelly bed with springs coming out of the mattress. I got my own kettle. The first thing I bought was a plate and a knife and fork – I chose them. The plate was white with pink spots. I became an independently living girl who didn't have to be in bed by ten o'clock. I had no-one to tell me what to do.'

'You know some of the story from hereon, Rosa. Little orphan Moira gets a job as a maid at the Sonny Mabon Associates building. As you know, a maid's got to be humble, not ask questions, say yes and no, and please, and thank you. A maid has to go about her business like she's invisible and be as quiet as a mouse; she has to respond to other's wishes and ensure that the wishes are fulfilled. Of course, not in the way that the girls in the cages fulfilled wishes, but she's still got to do her job and not give any cause for the management to get rid of her. Do you know, Rosa, I was a maid for close on two years, and scarcely anyone knew my name let alone anything about where I'd come from. That girl in the black and white uniform could have been from outer space – they didn't care so long as I did my job.'

'Then what... you come to work the cages. To me, you were just another glamorous girl with lots of self-confidence and lots of boldness. I didn't know exactly what the girls in the cages did, and I didn't wish to know. I saw them in the preparatory room, manacled to hooks on display, and sometimes I'd have to release them from gadgets after the clients had finished with them. I blocked all that stuff out of my mind and concentrated on being anonymous. Unseen, unheard Moira – that was me.'

'Then what... for the first time, I see a stranger's eyes trying to make contact. I'm kind of scared, embarrassed, even suspicious. Why is someone looking at me – I have nothing but a plate with pink spots. Don't those eyes know I'm a lonesome soul with not a single endearing quality? But you didn't give up, Rosa... you kept on looking, you'd say the odd words, I think one time you called me cute but I wasn't sure what you meant by cute. I thought you perhaps meant I was young and shouldn't be working at such a place as SMA. I used to go to my horrible room and think you must talk to all the maids in the same way. Surely, you couldn't just be looking at me.'

'Remember... remember when you put your hand under my skirt? I couldn't believe it. Someone had shown me affection, and then I crazily thought you were maybe offering to give me love for money. You girls worked for money. You couldn't possibly see me as attractive. I couldn't work out your motives, and I couldn't afford to pay you for being kind to me, not even for just being a friend.'

'From here you know the story, Rosa... I can't recall the precise details of how it went, but I came to live with you – was it a

day or two before Tracey… We both left SMA and I quit my life of
isolation. Oh, for a while, I didn't know what role I'd play. I'd be
anything you wanted me to be. You told me that you cared. You said
I was beautiful. You introduced me to sex, and God, I can't tell you
how astonishing it felt to be in the arms of someone who cared for
me. I can't tell you what I first thought of sex because I was lost in a
world I'd never encountered. Being touched gave me strange
sensations, wonderful sensations, but being loved gave me so much
more than you can ever know. And then came the Mum-bit. As well
as our bodies coming together, we had this kind of mother/daughter
relationship. When you cuddled me, I'd feel secure. Laying on your
breasts was the most glorious feeling of any. I started to call you
Mum because you seemed like a mum and I longed to be your
daughter. And in those moments when you didn't treat me like your
daughter, I wanted to be your lover – to give you as much pleasure as
you were giving me. I came to learn how you were so needy of sex
and promised myself that I would give you anything you desired from
me even though you received sex from others. Other folks, apart
from Tracey, were sex-partners, but they weren't your lover and your
daughter like me.'

'And for a while, everything was fine. Eventually, I let Tracey
touch me because I thought that the three of us making love would
please you, and I loved Tracey a little – I knew you loved her and
when the three of us had sex it was as if we were sharing our love.
That time when you and Tracey screwed me in your bed left me in no
doubt that I'd found happiness. We seemed devoted to each other. I
knew that you may go off occasionally to have sex elsewhere, but
nothing would ever destroy what we'd built.'

'Somehow, I knew that when Lizzie came along, you wouldn't
be able to resist her, and you'll recall how Lizzie wanted me but I saw
Lizzie as merely a friend. I'd have sex with you and Tracey, but not

with her. There came the instance of her assaulting me at the precinct. You put me and Lizzie on different shifts at the café. It doesn't take a genius to work out what's going to happen next. As I once overheard Tracey tell you, 'Lizzie is built for you, she's as hot as a minefield.' Very soon you'd be screwing Lizzie, but I knew that you didn't love her.'

'Anyhow, you're affair with Lizzie reached a peak when she tied you to the bed and beat your body so badly you were left black and blue. I and Tracey were in London. When I came home and saw you, I thought my world had ended. You invited Lizzie to live with us and I felt pushed out, but little orphan Moira wasn't going to lay down and die and lose the only person who's ever loved her. I'd battle to win your heart and Lizzie isn't going to replace me in your affections.'

Then what... weeks without sex, weeks seeing you look frustrated, weeks seeing frowns on your face and you appearing to cry without tears. It hurt knowing you're pained. Just like how you rescued me from SMA, I had to rescue you from a sex-free life. And if it meant me offering my body to Katy, Marty, Tracey, Lizzie, and you, effectively being gang-banged, then that's what I was prepared to do to return us all to happiness. You wanted to see me being gang-banged, didn't you?'

I try to interrupt, hold my hands out to Moira but she's not accepting excuses and sits further back on the sofa. She looks to the clock on the mantel, then continues with her speech.

'Sex begins again. We all screw Lizzie instead. Katy and Marty vanish. Tracey, Lizzie, you, and I end up in a foursome. Before the girls go to London, we seem to become two pairs. Tracey takes a shine to Lizzie, and we become permanent fixtures in your bed. Then what, Rosa...? I give up the daughter role completely and determine to become your full-time lover. If you want sex five times a day, I'll please you. If you want to screw me all day, I'm your servant. I'll take sex from you, and give you sex in equal measure. I'll be anything that you wish me to be, and even if you want to see me being screwed by men, I'll do that. I'll take real penises instead of dildo look-a-likes if that's what you want from me.'

I spring from the armchair and throw myself between Moira's knees. 'Don't be silly,' I say.

'You love me talking about strangers. You get off on it. You don't ask me what I want. You think you know what I want. My only desire is to please you but you can't help but step ahead of me to prepare what you think is my fantasy – you're convinced that my joys are your joys. Admit it, Rosa, you're lining me up to be gang-banged because you think it will be the biggest turn-on of your life.'

Truth wounds. I'm guilty and I plead forgiveness with wide-open eyes. I again try to hold Moira's hands but she pulls back her arms and half-screams that I don't ask what she wants – I assume things, I misinterpret her words, I add meaning to her pleasure of the penis-shaped dildo, I take her talk of strangers as gospel.

'Yesterday evening,' she says, 'when I laid you on my bed and kissed your neck until you fell asleep – wasn't that the most fabulous sex you've ever had? You swooned; you went to sleep in Heaven. And the day before when we had sex all over the house, weren't you thoroughly satisfied? Am I not enough for you, or must you screw everyone and have everyone screw me?'

'It's not like that,' I say.

Moira pushed my arms and knees to the side. She gets from the sofa and moves the clock on the mantel, turns quickly, and waves Joe's business card under my nose. 'That's what you've been searching for – sweet little Moira is ready for her gang-bang.'

'That's not true, 'I say.

'You have been searching for this!'

'Yes.'

'To arrange my deflowering!'

'I haven't called him.'

'You're lying – you have called him.'

'When?'

Moira snatches my phone from the chair arm then puts the business card close to my eyes. 'See all those sevens in the number?' she says pointedly. 'That's what I noticed when I found the card on the kitchen table. And do you remember, a while ago, when I needed to call the wholesalers and my phone hadn't been charged – you let me use your phone. I looked in the call log to search for the wholesaler's number; it wasn't there, but the number with all the sevens was there – you'd called Joe and arranged for me to be gang-banged, you just didn't know when and where!'

Jesus! I'd forgotten about call logs. I have to explain to Moira my guilty thoughts about arranging a gang-bang for myself – those baren weeks had got to me, I needed sex and Joe was the only person I could think of who'd be willing, along with his mates, to please me. I am a disgusting creature but I swear that I'd not called him with Moira in mind. She is correct in thinking that I do have fantasies and one of those is watching her have sex, and when she spoke about strangers and showed a fascination with the penis-like dildo I put two and two together and got five. I'm shameful, I'm a raving sex-maniac but she means more to me than anything. I'll listen to what she wants out of life. I'll adjust my behavior. I'm sorry, please forgive me. Moira says we'll talk tomorrow when we've both had time to digest this most meaningful conversation.

A look in the mirror

Self-castigation is fine if it's justified. I realize that I'm like many
other folks and just take from conversations those parts that I wish to
hear. I'm also guilty of thinking about me, what pleases me, what do
I do for excitement. Moira took a back seat; she gave her all but I
relegated her to an accessory. I deserve to be rolled into a ball and
sent hurling from a mountain summit to crash on the rocks in the
valley bottom.

Imagine, if I'd taken Moira to a hotel room and fed her to
masculine lust – 'Take no notice if she's crying, don't let her struggles
fool you – guys, give her your best and pulverize her innocence!'
She'd have never forgiven me. I'd be alone in the house and running
the café single-handed.

For the rest of the day speaking about our relationship was
taboo. Occasionally, she fired a look that asked me if I was doing
some serious thinking. My eyes told her, yes, and I hoped that she
believed me. And when she took me to her bed mid-evening, I felt
grateful for her attention.

Just as yesterday evening, she laid me on her bed and put her
finger to her lips. I hadn't to make a sound, simply lay there, and
accept her generosity – she was still giving, still trying to cement our
bond, and likely getting me valuing her more than I have.

She pushed up my top and lowered the waistband of my
skirt. At first, she ran her hands softly over my belly without ever
making eye-contact. Then she started to thrill my body with oh so
tiny kisses that brought unusual sensations to the surface of my skin.
And they gradually became proper kisses and sucks; she used her
tongue, made wiggly lines with her fingernails, and always stopped
just below my tits or just above my mound. It's like she was saying
'This is what I can do for you – there are more ways of delivering

eroticism than we've practiced: sex doesn't need to result in multiple orgasms. Girl, look what I'm doing to you, and you're not complaining.'

She thrilled me by making love to my belly. We ended up kissing and not an item of clothing had left our bodies. That night we slept in pajamas in my bed and my heart sizzled with love rather than passion.

A new dawn

After our shift at the café, we came home, changed out of our uniforms, and I can't say precisely how it came about, but we dressed in our underwear and bathrobes. I don't think either of us intended to have sex – it seemed a case of being on equal terms, as though we could have our forthcoming conversation with the protection of the bathrobe if it were needed.

Before we came downstairs, I put the cigarette lighter that we use to light the bedroom candles into my pocket along with Joe's business card and my mobile phone. We agreed to make a coffee, then I'd tell Moira what I'd been thinking about since yesterday.

We made the coffee. She looked a little scared and three of four times tightened her bathrobe belt. She had me thinking that she'd decided on something, and I've got to admit I felt worried. Then before we picked up the coffee cups, I opened the rear door and beckoned her to the doorway.

'I love you, Moira,' I say. She cups her arm under mine but chooses not to reply. 'I never thought, after Marty, I'd commit my body and soul to anyone. Sure, I love Tracey, and Tracey has been my friend, my lover, my partner in crime. But I and Tracey have never said that we'll be loyal to each other, not really meaning it, not

intending to eternally banish others from our bed. But you, Moira…
you are…'

Moira tightens her grip on my arm and expels a tiny laugh.
'And I seriously thought that I'd be Moira Saint John – your daughter.
I did. Honestly, I thought you'd be my ideal Mum – you'd tire of
having sex with me and go off having sex with anyone you could find.
It didn't bother me, as I saw it then, your lovers are temporary, but a
daughter is forever. You could have as much sex as you desire but it
won't affect us. You'll always be my Mum, and I'll be the winner.'

'And now… mother or lover?' I say.

'First Partner,' says Moira like it's a special title.

I feel relieved and take Joe's card from my pocket along with
the lighter. I hold the card at arm's length and set it on fire. We
watch it burn and as the flame closes on my fingers, I drop it to the
ground. We retreat to the kitchen and I pass Moira my phone.
'Delete the number from the call log – delete all the numbers you do
not recognize. There'll be no more gang-bangs, I promise.'

Moira hesitates; I nudge her and encourage her to proceed. I
point out Katy's number and other numbers worth saving. The
numbers of past lovers and Joe are swallowed into the phone's
darkness. We pick up our coffee cups and saunter into the room and
sit how we did before.

'I don't wish you to become anything other than that you
wish to be,' says Moira. I want you to differentiate between what I
may say to please you, and that which is genuinely me. I'm not
denying that I spoke about strangers or mentioned penises, but I
want neither. As far as guys go, I'm a virgin, your virgin, and that's
how I wish to remain. I may dream what it's like to have sex with
guys but dreams don't have to be realities. My reality is you. My
body is for you – I don't know where Tracey and Lizzie figure, I
haven't thought about it. I don't care if you have sex with the girls

when they come back from London or if we all have sex together. I
care about us, our boundaries, the distance, or lack of distance
between us. I don't want to be alone in my bed, I want us to be in
bed knowing that's the only place in the world where you or I wish to
be. I'll give you everything I have as I've tried to do since the girls
went. Sex no times a day, or ten times a day is no bother. I love
giving you orgasms and I love receiving them; so long as we're
together I don't give a damn what we do. Yesterday kissing your
belly, and the day before kissing your neck – we can do that, we can
do anything. I'll share with you all of my body and all of my love.'

'I'm sorry for what I've done,' I say. 'I took you for granted. I
put my thoughts into your head and believed they were your
thoughts. I even convinced myself that the jealousy I'd feel wouldn't
matter, and God, you've no idea how jealously possessive I am of
you. It killed me to see you offering your body to Katy, Marty,
Tracey, and Lizzie. When you said 'Mum' and allowed me to save
you, I felt wonderful. But when you said you'd sacrifice yourself to a
dozen strangers, I felt sexually aroused and dwelt on an image of
depravity that wouldn't go out of my head. I was stupid, selfish, and
wrong. Don't you know how I adore you as 'my sweet little virgin'
and to not be able to call you that would be heartbreaking? I'm
ashamed of my thoughts. I never asked Joe if he and his mates
would like to screw you, but the thought crossed my mind. Forgive
me, Moira.'

Moira gets up, sits on my knee. She tells me there is nothing
perverse about having fantasies of guys screwing her. We can talk
about them, say dirty things when we're having sex – thinking is free,
and she confesses to wondering what was done to me when I worked
the cages, someday I can tell her, and we can attempt to recreate
those sex acts, however naughty, however indecent they were.

We start kissing then pushing each other's bathrobe from the shoulders. Moira says she'd like me to tie her to our bed or maybe put her in Marty's pink straps. She is not averse to being screwed all afternoon, and it's time I paid her back for the glorious kissing of my neck and belly, preferably… she laughs again… with a lot of use of the penis-like dildo affixed to the strap-on belt.

I look lovingly into her eyes and marvel at her beauty. 'My sweet little virgin, I'll do more things to your body than any dozen guys ever could.'

A crazy few days

Not since I first set up home with Marty all those years ago, have I felt such calm and gazed into the future with such high hopes of happiness knitting the years ahead. We told Tracey and Lizzie of our commitment when they called. It seems like Tracey is similarly falling for Lizzie; they aren't averse to keeping the foursomes going providing they will be exceptions rather than the rule. They're delighted to know that I've vowed to curtail my wanderings and treat Moira with the respect she deserves.

When they said 'respect', Moira and I howled with laughter. If they could have watched us during the days that followed, they'd have witnessed the most shocking scenes of their lives. Moira and I didn't have sex, we became sex, sometimes screwing each other so ferociously or so gorgeously for hours on end that we fell asleep on each other. We stunk the house out, and as soon as we'd disinfected everywhere, we'd screw again as if we were competing to be the givers and receivers of most orgasms in a lifetime. We desired to prove that we'd never tire of worshiping the other's body.

We played all kinds of silly games, one in which Moira would yell 'Mum' throughout our screwing, and another when I'd tell Moira about sex acts in the rooms at SMA. We talked dirty, we gagged each other so we couldn't talk, we bound each other, we had sex in every position previously known to humankind – and we thought of other positions, and other depraved sex acts that even the devil doesn't consider decent. Some of our inventions blew our minds and others were complete disasters. And all the while we mixed sex with love, never going more than a few minutes without tender words, never failing to express our love when cooking, cleaning, or between serving customers at the café.

And that first Sunday after our conversations proved to be among the best days of my life. I think from around nine on the previous evening we scarcely paused from having sex until around eleven on Sunday evening. Some folks may say that's a bit excessive as well as impossible; I could argue that it's excessive but I know for sure it's not impossible. I would guess that Moira and I must have lost 10lbs between us during the work-out and we both looked fabulous afterward.

And the changes came one by one

I suppose there's a moment after folks quit drinking or smoking when they realize they've conquered the addiction. My moment came sooner than expected, only days after committing to Moira, a list of reserve sex-partners got erased from my mind. There were blank spaces where names such as Uncle Russia, Kev and Timmy, Lucy, Jake, and Hallie used to be. If I wasn't thinking of sex with Moira, then I wasn't thinking of sex, period.

But let's begin at the café... we started to accept that the café is our place of work and for five hours each morning we put our desires on hold and served breakfasts and hot food sandwiches as they do in any respectable establishment. No groping behind the counter, no laying Moira on top of the freezer, or closing the shutters early to have sex on a table. And our attitude to customers took a turn for the better; more chats, more letting them see we were a pair of normal girls and we held opinions about the weather and were capable of offering sympathy, smiles, advice, or whatever was asked of us. Many of the regulars began to see beyond the sexy uniforms and took to saying, 'Morning, Rosa' or 'Morning, Moira', and the sexual innuendoes just about disappeared. It's amazing how guys quickly differentiate between girls with hot bodies and those simply doing a job. I guess for the first time I wasn't permanently preoccupied with sex.

After work, one or two days a week, we'd go for a ride in the van to no particular destination. There'd be 30-mile journeys on country roads or sometimes we'd head up the motorway to a junction or two further north, then get lost and have fun finding our way back to East Leeds. Other days, we'd return home, change our clothes, and go to town on the bus. We'd visit clothes stores, buy perfumes or games for Moira, or shoes or sexy underwear. We even called in café's or wine bars but only to rest our legs.

One of the most significant changes was our regular visits to Katy and Marty's house or my parents. I think the visits began because I wanted to exhibit my happiness to folks who knew me well, and on Katy's part, she was mightily relieved to learn that I intended Moira to be my everlasting partner. Katy even had her girls calling Moira 'Aunty' and Moira got on with the girls splendidly. Marty was resigned to the fact that our relationship lay in the past. He once joked that we should sit in their room and watch the full version of the Golf Club gang-bang but Katy soon put him in his place and said such a thing was insensitive.

We often spent an hour or two chatting without me ever thinking about sneaking Katy upstairs and molesting her body in the shower. However, we spent even more hours gossiping with my parents. They'd not just welcomed their youngest daughter back to the fold, they gained an extra daughter in Moira. And boy, did they love Moira! In mother and father's eyes, Moira is about twelve years old and they simply refuse to believe that she can be my lover. 'She's the sweetest of the lot of you,' mother would say. And father didn't cast his lecherous looks at her as he often did to me when I wore tarty clothing. Father would warn Moira to 'watch her'. And say, 'Our Rosa has motives' as if I were trying to get Moira into bed. I'd tell him that we're full-blown lesbians but he didn't pay attention. Both of my parents offered Moira sweeties as if she could take the gifts to her school and share them with classmates. Moira felt amused by their parental affection and she has grown to think of them as grandparents.

Another couple we bumped into occasionally was Sally and Harry. We'd see them at the local shop or in the park. They were talkative, and there were no awkward moments. Harry had returned to his full set of hours at work and Sally was absorbed in the joys of motherhood. She always insisted on taking the child from the pushchair and then introducing the toddler to her friends, Rosa, and Moira. She hadn't got her beautiful figure back but it would have made no difference if she had. Rosa Saint John's eyes weren't straying from her super-gorgeous partner who stood at her side holding her hand.

And that brings me to the dynamics that altered my thinking and how I transformed from being a sexual predator into a girl wholly content with life. Oh, I've been in love before... with Marty, and my love for Marty had been true. In those days I had a naïve view of life – shack up, live, and die together no matter what circumstances developed. He cheated on me. I found Tracey Cummings who introduced me to sex. I fell in love with Tracey but sex always seemed more important than love, and now there is love but infrequent sex. She hasn't cheated on me but she's found the balance which is 50% love and 50% sex with Lizzie. I hope they'll be happy.

With Moira, I have the best of everything. I love her and she loves me. I invest all my fantasies in her body. My urges to wander are no more. We are used to each other's ways. We desire each other's flesh. Our eyes sparkle when we glimpse each other, and as we stare. There is a union of hearts and minds and all we share is perfectly balanced.

I have learned that my travels are ended and with them go my confessions. Tomorrow I shall be with Moira, and with her for all the years that follow. I am back to my starting point but with an abundance of experiences and memories. When Tracey and Lizzie return, I am sure we'll reside in this house as a family, but as a family with two distinct couples. Each one of us has ascended from a darker past – two orphans and two former whores who through Tracey's hard work and ingenuity shall step forward into harmony and prosperity without the need to look over our shoulders and believe anything is missing from life. We shall have it all. We have our love, our beds, and if we require them, our two drawers filled with sex toys. No more confessions. Moira awaits me in our bed of never-ending joy. Goodnight X.

The End.

A review of Amazon would be very much appreciated. Thank you.

www.ingramcontent.com/pod-product-compliance
Lightning Source LLC
Chambersburg PA
CBHW071620150726
48000CB00004B/1803